To my grandchildren who are yet
to travel to their high places

Felix Publishing 2025
email: info@felixpublishing.com
Print copies also available from the publisher.

Where Condors Soar – Tales from Old South America

2025 digital book release
ISBN: 978-1-92566255-9
Print Edition
ISBN: 978-1-92566254-2
Author: Peter T. Scott

Registration:
Thorpe-Bowker +61 3 8517 8342
email: bowkerlink@thorpe.com.au

No part of this publication may be reproduced, stored in a retrieval system, or transmitted in any form or by any means, electronic, mechanical, photocopying, recording or otherwise, without the prior written permission of the publisher.

This is a work of fiction. The characters in this book did not exist and the politics of the time has been generalized. Some of the places described are real and are well-known to the author. No disrespect is meant to any people living or dead in the countries of South America for which the author has a great love.

© All rights reserved Felix Publishing
2025

Other Fiction by the Author

South American Historical Adventures (as Hernan Moreno Ruiz)
    Letters from San Rafael
    Return to San Rafael
    Confessions of Father Xavier

Science Fiction
    The Ice Ship
    200 Years Before the Mast
    Orion and Other Stories of the Future
    Poseidon's People

Humour
    The Innocence of Tom Shipley: Teacher.
    Tom Shipley's War: Memoirs of a Weekend Warrior.

Australiana
    The Cry of the Currawong

Supernatural Crime (Omnibus Editions)
    The Casebook of the Ghost and Detective McNab
    More from the Casebook of the Ghost and Detective McNab

The author also has written many works of non-fiction in the Earth Sciences, Environmental Sciences, Teaching and Survival genres as both Print and eBooks.

Where
Condors Soar

Tales from Old South America

Peter T. Scott

First released 2025

MAR CARIBE
MAPA 1
COLOMBIA
Quit
Quito
ECUADOR
Guayaquil
Iquitos
Manaus
Santarém
MAP 2
PERU
Lima
Cuzco
Andes
La Paz
BOLIVIA
Altiplano
BRAZIL
PARAGUAY
Antofagasta
Rio de Janeiro
CHILE
MAPA 3
Pampas
URUGUAY
Mercedes
Buenos Aires
ARGENTINA
Andes
OCÉANO PACÍFICO
OCÉANO ATLÁNTICO
Ushuaia
Tierra del Fuego
SUDAMERICA
1886
SCALE 1:35,000,000

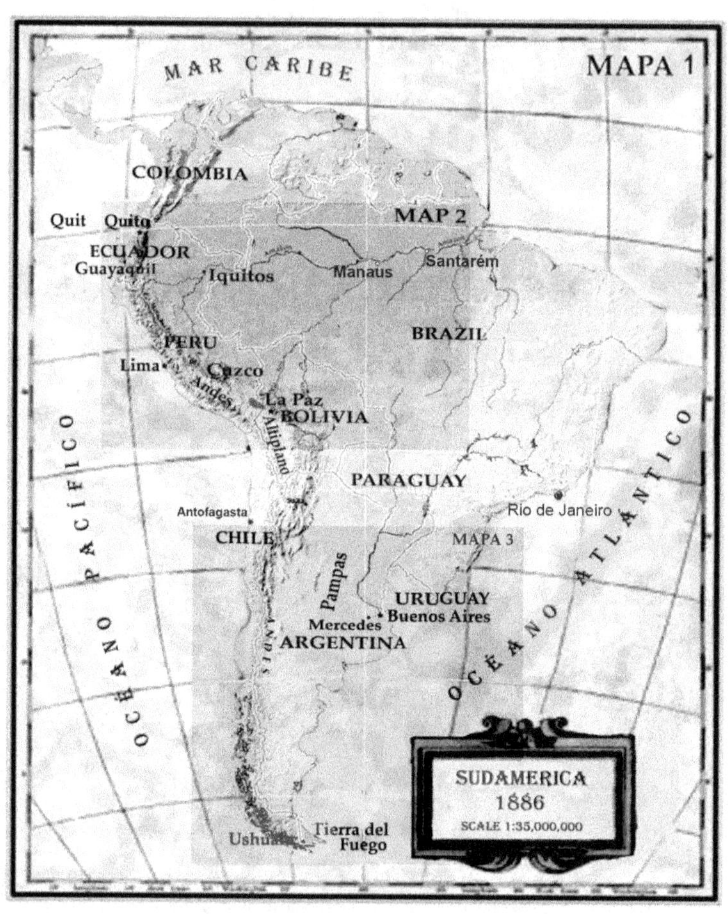

i

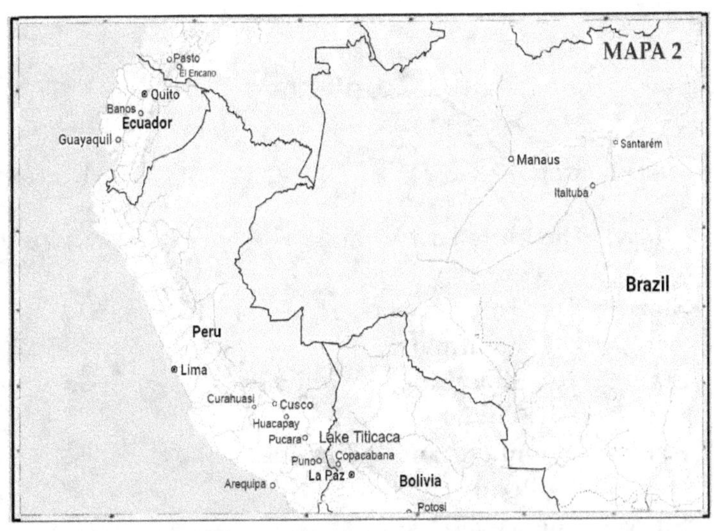

MAPA 2
Pasto
El Encano
Quito
Banos
Ecuador
Guayaquil
Manaus
Santarém
Italtuba
Brazil
Peru
Lima
Curahuasi
Cusco
Huacapay
Pucara
Lake Titicaca
Puno
Copacabana
La Paz
Arequipa
Bolivia
Potosi

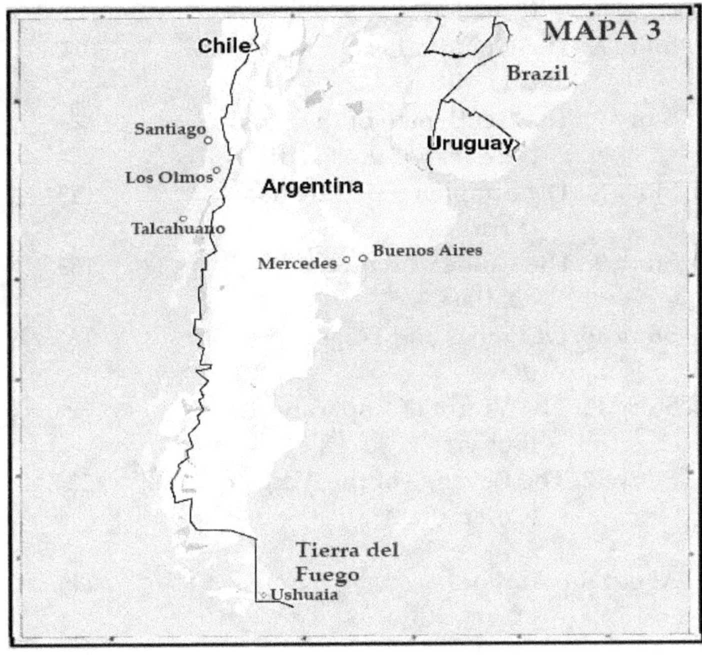

MAPA 3
Chile
Brazil
Santiago
Uruguay
Los Olmos
Argentina
Talcahuano
Mercedes
Buenos Aires
Tierra del
Fuego
Ushuaia

Contents

Introduction

This is a book of short stories set in South America at the end of the nineteenth century – a time when most countries are trying to establish themselves after the quarrels following independence from Spain and Portugal. In the second half of that century, wars had been fought between Ecuador and Peru, there had been civil wars in Argentina and Peru and Bolivia had been defeated in the War of the Pacific with Chile.

But many of these stories are not about war but about the people and events of that time. Some stories come from the myths and religious beliefs of the people; others from real events and some have been taken from things which I have observed in my extensive travels around that continent. These stories have been mostly taken and re-written from my books *LETTERS from SAN RAFAEL, RETURN to SAN RAFAEL* and *CONFESSIONS of FATHER XAVIER* which were written under my nom de plume of Hernan Moreno Ruiz, the main character of the first two novels. In these books, these stories are highly integrated within the action of these historical adventures and involve the main characters in the novels. I encourage the reader to now find and read these books to get a wider view of the life and times of that wonderful continent. In many places I have given some colloquial expressions in Spanish except for Story Six which is set in Brazil and so the terms are given in Portuguese.

Peter T. Scott
2025

Story One:

The Little Lost Alpaca
(La Pequeña Alpaca Perdida)

This is a story for children. It is about a small boy and his pet alpaca who live with their family high in the Altiplano of Peru.

It was mid-morning and a beautiful day. Summer had arrived and the smile of Inti the sun beamed down on the people of the high mountains of the Andes. It threw long shadows from the colonnades surrounding the small garden of the cathedral in the city of Lima on the central coast of Peru. The old priest sat on a stone bench surrounded by a small group of very young children from the orphanage. He was recounting a story to the children, and this is what he said:

"Let me tell you, my children, of a little boy much like you, Americo," he said, pointing to the oldest boy. "He lived in southern Peru – my country – in a valley in the mountains where the condors soar high in the sky.

"What is a condor, Padre Pablo?" said one of the smaller girls, whose name was Florencia.

"Condors are the giant birds which fly very high in the mountains, the ancient people who lived there believed them to be sacred. They thought that these giant birds were the messengers from Heaven[1]." The old priest smiled and continued: "But let me tell you about Antonio who lived on a farm in the mountains not far from the big lake where it is thought that the ancient people came from."

"What is a lake, Padre Pablo?" asked Florencia again, as she was always full of questions and the other children laughed.

[1] *In the ancient Quechua language of the Incas, these birds were called 'Kuntur' and were thought to be the messengers between the upper world* (Hanan Pacha) and their earthly world (Kay Pacha).

"Well. My child" Padre Pablo continued. "It is a very large, flat amount of water. It is a wide valley filled with water which takes a long while to cross if you have a boat. You can just see the high mountains on the other side. It is called 'Lago Titicaca[2]' and it is very big. I was there when I was but a boy like Americo here, many years ago. I stayed with the people in the mountains."

"Did you go on a boat?" Padre Pablo?" asked Andrés, his dark black hair hanging down over his broad, brown face.

"Ah, no, Andrés. We were too busy for that. But the people who live there build boats out of woven reeds from the lake, which float very well. These people are called 'Los Uros',[3] they

[2] *From the old name 'Titiq'aq'a' given by the Aymara people who still live on its southern shores in Peru and Bolivia, meaning 'grey puma' because on a map and looking from the west it looks like a crouching puma*
[3] *The Uros people who still live on the Lake although under modern conditions with their traditional houses and customs displayed for tourists*

live in reed houses built on floating islands of the same reed well away from others who might harm them. But let us return to the farm in the mountains.

It is much higher there than in your mountains here where there are trees and green plants everywhere. In his mountains, little Antonio – for that was the name of the boy in our story – there were very few trees and bushes and even those were very small. But there was much grass and many small shrubs and so the people on the shores of the lake and higher in the mountains which surround it, built their houses out of stone and adobe."

"What is adobe?" interjected Antonio the curious.

"Mud, my little friend. Mud. The people make mud using the soil near their home and water from the river. They make a big puddle of mud. Have you not made mud puddles, Americo?"

"Oh, si, Padre Pablo. Many times, and we get very dirty and Sister Josefina scolds us and makes us have a wash in the cold river!"

"Well, the people in the mountains would also get very dirty and they too would then have to wash in the river at the end of the day. But during morning they mix straw or grass with the mud and push it into little wooden boxes which give the mud its shape. They squeeze the water out and then tip the box upside down so that the mud falls out. They then lay it out on the ground in the sun and let it dry. This is an adobe brick. They work very hard, with the family all working together; the adults and all of the children too. After many days they have hundreds of bricks, so they then can build their houses."

"We build our houses out of wood," said Lucia, one of the smaller girls.

"Our house is made of stone like the cathedral" said Andrés with some pride.

"Well, there certainly are many stones in the mountains," replied the priest. "Many people build their houses out of stone there too. Especially up in the hills where there is little soil but many stones. But to continue the story", giving Andrés a stern look which changed to a grin.

" The house that little Antonio lived in was made of brown adobe bricks. Antonio lived with his Papa Alberto and Mama Isadora and his brothers Santiago and Jorge and his sister little Gabriella. His abuelo[4], Don Tomás and his abuela[5], Doña Agustina also lived with the family and it was Don Tomás and his friends who started the building many years ago.

Now listen, children! These farmhouses are not like the ones around here in these narrow valleys where there is little room. Here you may have one small house. Some in the town, I am told even has two heights. In Antonio's

[4] *Grandfather*
[5] *Grandmother*

mountains, where they can find some land which is flat, perhaps near a stream, they will build several small houses close together. They then connect the house with walls about as high as a man. They are also made from adobe bricks, so that a courtyard is formed. It would probably be as big as this courtyard." The old priest gestured with a sweep of his arm. "The houses would have windows and doors facing into the centre like those here in the courtyard, but their houses usually would not have an upstairs. Although in some places, farmers who are very prosperous, and build their houses out of stone might build a bigger house with an upstairs room where the family live, and with a space below to put their animals. However, Antonio's farm only had a house with no upstairs. They had one house with two rooms for papa and mama and the children, another small house for Abuelo Tomás and Abuela Agustina and a third even smaller house for the family to cook and eat their food. There was also a small open shelter running along one wall for the animals."

"Where was the baños[6]?" cried out little Manuela with a look of concern on her little round face.

"Do not worry, my child." Padre Pablo continued. "Outside, behind the courtyard, Abuelo Tomás had built a fine little building which contains the toilet and shelter which had a water drum and wash basin.

Now, wood was scarce in the mountains and was used only in making the two big gates for the courtyard, the frames for the rooves and the shutters for the windows – not to mention the few pieces of furniture, of course – the rooves were all made of tightly plaited straw called thatch. This made the houses very warm at night and kept out the rain, although it did not rain often in these dry mountains.

Now, can you guess what was placed on top of the rooves, children?" Roberto looked around with a broad smile and eyes wide open.

[6] *The word 'baños' has several meanings in Spanish. Used for the name of the nearby town, it means 'bath' like the city in England, but it could also mean 'washroom' or 'toilet'.*

The children all looked perplexed and found an answer very difficult.

"Rocks!" spoke up Antonio, who definitely was the leader of the group because he was the eldest. "In the town I have seen people put rocks on the roof so that the wind does not blow away the slabs of wood on their roof."

"Fray Dominic has a cross on his roof. He pointed to it when Sister Josefina and I took some things to his Mission." Spoke little Lucia, her eyes wide with anticipation that her answer would be the correct one.

"Ah, very close, my child. On all of the rooves in Antonio's farm indeed was a cross but also two little bulls made out of baked clay," Padre Pablo replied quietly.

"Two bulls!" Andrés exclaimed. "They would be too heavy, and why did they put bulls on the roof?"

"They are only little clay bulls, Andrés," the old priest said with a grin. "Very nicely painted in many colours and put onto the very top and centre part of the roof. They are called 'Torita de

Pucará',[7] and they, and the cross, are there to bring good luck to all who live below the rooves.

Now that you know about the family and their house, let us return to little Antonio and his story, because it teaches us a very important lesson." Padre Pablo said pointing with his hand to nothing in particular. He continued his story:

"It had been a very good year for Papa Alberto; the maize grew high, and his potato crop all came up and he had more than enough potatoes for his family to eat. Now Abuelo Tomás and

---

[7] *Meaning 'little or young bulls of the town of Pucará'. A myth tells that in a great drought came upon Pucará, a small town just north of Lake Titicaca. To help the people of the district, a young farmer took a little bull upon his shoulders and climbed a nearby mountain hoping to sacrifice the animal to the Incan god Pacha Kamaq (Quechua "Creator of the World"). The bull resisted and fell off the man's shoulders and his horns struck the ground from which water now flowed. The drought had been broken. Now the bulls are still placed on some rooves for good luck and fertility of the soil.*

Papa Alberto could make much chicha[8] and Mama Isadora and Abuela Agustina would make many lovely hot roasted potatoes.

Now because they had more potatoes than their family and friends could eat, Papa Alberto decided to preserve much of his crop by making chuño[9]. This is the way that the Old People would make their crops last a very long time – even for many years! They would take their potatoes high into the cold mountains and spread the potatoes out on the ground. At night the potatoes would freeze. The next morning in the sun the potatoes would soften and then people would tread out all of the moisture from them. They would leave them to freeze again and then tread out the moisture again. After about five days, the potatoes became black and very dry."

[8] *A beer made from fermented maize.*
[9] *A method of freeze-drying from Quechua ch'uñu, meaning 'frozen potato'*

"Oh, but that would not taste very nice." Said little Sofia, who often helped Maria the cook in the orphanage.

"You eat many potatoes here in Lima, do you not, little one?" Padre Pablo replied. "I saw many potato fields on the sides of the hills when we first came here. Does not the good Maria cook many dishes with potatoes? Well, Mama Isadora and Abuela Agustina would take the chuño and use it in soups, cakes from its flour and even some sweet desserts.

So one day, Papa Alberto gathered all of his llamas,[10] then he and Abuelo Tomás loaded their packs with all of their extra potatoes ready to take them higher up the mountains to where they would make the chuño. Now think of how high that would be! Their farm was already

---

[10] *Pronounced 'lyamma' with emphases on the 'y' is a Camelid, that is a member of the family of camels which first appeared in North America about 45 million years ago and spread to South America and Asia. In the Americas they are found in in the Andes from southern Ecuador to Bolivia and include domesticated llamas and alpacas and the wild vicuñas and guanacos.*

twice as high as we are now and around the farm were many tall mountains so high that the snow on their tops did not melt, even during summer. It would take them several days to get to their favourite spot on the mountains and so they also took other food, blanket, and other things which they would need for a week in the cold mountains."

"What is a llama?" little Mariangeles, the smallest girl in the group asked.

The old priest answered softly. "In the country, up in the high mountains live the llamas. They are beautiful animals with brown or white bodies covered in soft wool, tall necks about the height of a man. They are used to carry many things from one place to another."

"I know all about llamas!" Andrés exclaimed. "Fray Dominic told me about them and showed me a drawing of one in his book. They live in the desert and are very clever."

"That is true." Padre Pablo replied. They do like the desert. It is much too wet down here on this side of the mountains. They like to be high in the dry air. The Old People took their wild ancestors from the desert and made them their own animals to carry their belongings. Since then, the people of the high mountains have also done so. The llamas also have some smaller cousins; the little alpaca who has very soft wool from which we make our warm clothing and blankets and the bigger wild guanaco and their smaller relatives the vicuñas. They live in the high mountains, but I have not seen any near Lima and they would not like to live here. It is too wet.

Now…where was I? Ah, yes. Now Antonio had a little pet alpaca which he called Sumaq,[11] and because Antonio had turned twelve years of age, Papa Alberto decided that he too should also come on the trip to the mountains so that he could learn how to make chuño and how to live in the mountains.

Papa Alberto looked at his son with a stern face and reminded him that llamas were sacred

11 *Quechua feminine name meaning "beautiful".*

animals, and that the family depended upon them to carry their potatoes to the high valleys to make chuño and to the markets. Without the llamas, the people of the high mountains would have a very difficult life. Papa Alberto had made a little bridle to put around Sumaq's neck so that Antonio could lead him along the mountain paths like Papa Alberto did with the adult llamas.

'You must never lose your little alpaca in the high mountains.' Papa Alberto said sternly to Antonio. 'Keep her well protected and treat her like your very own child. You must look after her all of the time, and God and Urcuchillay[12] will watch over you both.' These were the words that Papa Alberto spoke to his son.

Early the next morning, just as Inti the sun came up over the mountains, Papa Alberto and Abuelo Tomás loaded their potatoes into the

[12] *Urcuchillay [Quechua: 'Urch-chil-AY'] was a god worshipped by Incas herders, who was believed to take the shape of a multi-coloured llama who watched over animals.*

baskets which were carried on both sides of each llama except for the lead llama whose name was Sinchi[13]. On his back were the items needed to stay several nights in the mountains; some food, warm clothing, blankets for the night chill and some sticks with which to start their fires – although there would be some old vicuña dung along the trail which burns very nicely.

So off they went. Papa Alberto went first leading Sinchi by his head collar rope and the others following with their head ropes tied to the harness of the one in front. Abuelo Tomás followed in the rear with his colourful q'ipirina[14] on his back and his long walking stick with the head of the sacred puma carved at its top. Antonio and Sumaq were allowed to walk with Papa Alberto at the very front of the llama train, much to Sinchi's annoyance. Sumaq thought that she was indeed beautiful, but Sinchi just

[13] *Quechua for "boss" or "leader"*
[14] *Quechua term for a woven blanket tied in a triangle and carried on the back as a pack.*

put his nose in the air and gave a superior snort of disapproval. Antonio and the men wore hand-woven trousers made from alpaca wool and thick ponchos[15] to keep the cold out. On their feet they wore sturdy leather ajotas[16] with tough soles for walking on the rocks. Antonio and Abuelo Tomás wore the traditional chullo[17] which were made from knitted alpaca wool, but Papa Alberto also wore a wide sombrero on top of his chullo.

They travelled all morning across the dry valley with many stones and a few small tuffs of grass and low shrubs and up onto one of the many ridges which ran parallel to the great range of snow-capped mountains in the distance. On top of one of the ridges, which Papa called el

[15] *A thick, woven cape worn over the shoulders with a hole for the head*
[16] *Sandals which cover most of the feet, now often made from rubber.*
[17] *From Aymara: 'ch'ullu', these are knitted hats with earflaps. The first chullo that a child receives is traditionally knitted by his father*

Mirador del Cielo[18], they stopped for a lunch of small cakes made by Abuela Agustina and water from the water skin tied to Sinchi's harness. They sat upon the ground where the stones had been cleared. The llamas were released to graze on the small tuffs of grass nearby. Antonio noticed that near where they sat were many tall piles of tiny stones which were stacked one upon the other. They looked like many small towers that consisted of about five or six rounded stones piled up with the largest on the bottom and the smallest on top. Papa Alberto explained that these piles of stones were called 'apachetas',[19] and were built by travellers as they climbed the trail. He said that as they walked the trail, they would pick up a small stone and carry it for a short distance to the top of the ridge. They would then add the stone to an existing apacheta. With this papa

[18] *Spanish: 'the lookout of the sky'*
[19] *From the Quechua and Aymara: word 'apachite', these small pebble towers not only acted as trail markers and campsites but some say that they were also places of the spirits called 'huacas', the stones being piled as thanks to Pachamama the earth goddess and Apu the god of the mountains for protection.*

Alberto took a small stone out of his pocket and carefully added it to the smallest apacheta nearby. 'Just for luck.' He said with a smile.

Antonio looked around at the wide view he had of the mountains and the valley. Back where they had come from and north of their trail was a broad, flat plain containing a salina[20] with a small lake. In the water was a small flock of flamingos.

Do you know what flamingos are?" Padre Pablo asked the children. They all shook their heads suggesting that they did not, so Padre Pablo continued: "They are large pink and white birds with long skinny legs. They like to walk in the waters of the salinas with their beaks upside down to catch the small creatures which live in the saltwater. Some say that their pink colour is caused by these little pink creatures which they eat."

[20] *A salt-lake or flats formed by the hot, volcanic springs along the altiplano*

"Then Florencia will turn yellow because she eats many bananas" interjected Andrés with a grin. The children laughed at this idea, even little Mariangeles who was a good-natured soul, laughed too.

"Perhaps," continued Padre Pablo." Her face looks nice and pink to me and flamingos are very beautiful. All of the children laughed, and Florencia flushed an even deeper shade of pink.

The old priest continued his story. "Higher up the trail, on another ridge, Antonio saw a small herd of vicuña. They were smaller than the llamas and their wool was shorter and a light brown in colour except for white tuffs below their necks and body. 'Look Papa, vicuñas!' Antonio exclaimed. Papa nodded and smiled and said that they had come from the salina in the valley where they licked salt and were now going up into the mountains to their high pastures. Sumaq thought that they were very handsome, and they were free to roam the mountains. She was very envious. Sinchi put his nose in the air and gave a superior snort." The children all laughed.

"So, after lunch had been taken, Papa Alberto collected all the llamas and tied their ropes one after each other and then to Sinchi's harness and then they again set off up the trail towards the high mountains.

It was very late in the afternoon and Inti the sun had hidden behind the snow-capped peaks in front of their trail. By now they were in another wide valley with very steep sides of bare rock, small slopes where the rocks had slipped down and sometimes grass where mountain springs trickled from the walls. Up the valley the peaks seemed to be higher and covered in more snow. Antonio could also see a little river of ice coming from a flat field of snow which had formed on the side of the tallest mountain. There were many smaller valleys going this way and that and a little river gurgled its way over a bed of large rocks down the valley from where they had come.

Eventually they stopped where a wide circle had been cleared in the stones and boulders of the valley floor near the trail. This circle had been used many times by travellers along the trail, it was a good place to sleep. There was a small circular pen made from rocks into which Papa Alberto herded the llamas. Little Sumaq was afraid to go into the small pen with the big llamas, so she was allowed to stay outside. But now Papa Alberto gave Antonio some very firm instructions.

'You must care for your alpaca. Tie her securely to one of the Keñua[21] bushes so that she does not run away, but give her some extra rope so that she can lie down.'

Antonio tethered his little alpaca under a bush and gave her a hug and wished her a good night sleep. He then walked along the trail looking for

[21] *Small shrubs with a twisted brown trunk and stubby branches with clumps of dark green leaves. They can be found over 5000 m as smaller bushes but are usually bigger at lower altitudes.*

dried dung for the fire which Abuelo Tomás had started with sticks in a small stone fireplace at the edge of their sleeping circle. Soon he had cooked a fine stew made from dried potatoes and corn, beans and chillies and a little charqui which, is dried meat. All of this he had carried on his back in his q'ipirina.

It was cold and the darkness of the night had closed in around them. The warm glow of the fire gave them some warmth and comfort. Papa Alberto had cut some of the tufts of ichu[22] grass and spread it on one side of the circle for their bed. Onto this he spread one of the woven blankets that Mama Isadora had made. They would be warm tonight, huddled together under their blankets.

After cleaning their plates and packing their supplies back into the packs, Papa Alberto said prayers to God and the Virgin for the family

[22] *A thin grass, often called 'feather grass' which grows in large clumps high in the Andes and is a source of food for the vicuñas and guanacos.*

back home and for their safe journey the next day. Then they pulled up their blankets and went to sleep. Antonio lay down and looked up at the clear dark sky with its sparkling cover of stars with the cold night wind blowing gently on his face. He looked up and saw the great river of stars called by the Old People 'Mayu', which we call the Milky Way. Abuelo Tomás was already softly snoring, so Antonio rolled over and went to sleep.

Now there was something that woke little Antonio sometime later, His father and grandfather were still fast asleep. The sky was still clear but now Mama Killa's[23] face shone fully on the country so Antonio could see the whole valley and the moonlight sparkled on the snowy white peaks of the mountains. Something was wrong but he did not know what it was. He quietly moved his blankets and crept away from his father's side. He put on his sandals, poncho and warm chullo and climbed up onto a rock at the edge of their sleeping

[23] *Quechua mama mother, killa moon, "Mother Moon"*

circle. He looked at the rock pen where the llamas were sleeping, and all was quiet. He looked over to the bush where Sumaq was sleeping. She was not there! Where had she gone, children?"

The children looked at each other and Andrés shrugged his shoulders and pouted. Little Sofia said, "She might have gone home to her mama?"

"But no, she did not go back down the valley to her mama. Where could she have gone?" asked Padre Pablo.

"She has run off to join the wild vicuñas" snorted Sinchi, his head now resting on the top stones of the pen, but all Antonio heard was his snorting and a series of trilled hoots.

"Antonio was very afraid for little Sumaq. She had broken her rope and had run away. Alpacas sometimes do that if they are not kept in their pen." continued Padre Pablo.

Now Antonio was a very smart boy. He also thought that Sumaq may have gone to look for the wild vicuñas which they had seen earlier going up into the mountains to their high pastures. He thought that Sumaq was a naughty alpaca and blamed himself for not tying the rope strongly. But what should he do? Should he wake Papa Alberto and Abuelo Tomás and get them to look for Sumaq? No! Antonio had been told by his father that Sumaq was his responsibility and must be cared for at all times. So, Antonio did a foolish thing. He decided to go and look for his little lost alpaca. After all, the Moon was full and bright, and he could see for a long way. Perhaps she is just over that ridge he thought. So, he quietly crept away from the sleeping circle and carefully treaded his way between the stones and the tufts of grass and began to climb the slope up to the ridge. It was a long climb because there was no trail. There were many large rocks which had rolled down from the tall peaks above and many thorny bushes and small cacti. Eventually Antonio reached the top and looked around. The brightness of Mama Killa allowed him to see a long way up the valley but there was no sign of Sumaq. Perhaps she went down the valley, he thought. No. She would climb higher to look for the vicuñas, so Antonio slowly headed along the ridge higher into the steep valley.

When he thought that he would not be heard by his father and grandfather, he called out 'Sumaq! Sumaq! But there was nothing except the gentle sound of the wind blowing down the valley.

Antonio was so concerned for his little alpaca that he did not think that this was a dangerous place. There were snakes and spiders, and sometimes even pumas, the big cats, would come up into the high mountains looking for young vicuñas. So, Antonio kept on walking. Up the valley, over the rocks which had fallen, and through the thorny bushes. Once he even came upon a small patch of snow and ice which had not melted because it was always in shadow, he carefully trod across the glistening white surface; each foot being placed flat upon the surface so he would not slip. He did not know how long he had been walking but now he was very uncertain as to where he was. 'Sumaq! Sumaq! He called, but still there was only the sound of Wayra the wind".

The children all huddled closer together and Antonio held little Mariangeles tightly. Padre Pablo continued:

"Now Sumaq had indeed found the small herd of vicuñas high up on the ridge. They had settled down for the night and were all fast asleep – except for the biggest vicuña who always kept one eye open for danger. He saw little Sumaq coming up the ridge, so he jumped up and gave a warning snort, wagging his tail so that his whole body shook. Sumaq stopped suddenly and gave a reassuring call which was like a low humming sound as if to say, 'May I come and join your herd?' The vicuñas were all awake and standing now and they looked at little Sumaq with very dark expressions."

Padre Pablo pulled a deep frown and looked around at the children who all laughed. He then continued his story by making sounds like those that vicuñas make when distressed – a series of high-pitched sounds. "Squeeku, squeeku, squeeku" the old priest said in a loud voice which again brought laughter from the children.

"The vicuñas quickly ran off a short distance then stopped and again looked at Sumaq. 'Go away. You are just a little alpaca and belong to the Humans. You are not a mountain vicuña.' They said and turned to run off over the ridge.

Little Sumaq was sad and felt very unwanted. She had so much wanted to be a vicuña and roam free in the mountains. But they were right. She was only a little alpaca and could never be a wild vicuña and roam the mountains. She suddenly felt afraid and lonely.

Just then, a long way off down the valley in the clear air she heard her name. 'Sumaq! Sumaq!' It was her Boy calling her. What was he doing up on the ridge? Here was someone who did want her, so she quickly turned and ran along the ridge down the valley.

Antonio was down in the valley and a long way from where his father and grandfather were sleeping. In fact, he was not sure where he was. He only knew that he was lost and cold. He was very sad. He had lost his little alpaca Sumaq and now he too was lost. The wind was now colder and coming off the snow of the high peaks up the valley.

He sat down upon a small rock and pulled his chullo down around his ears and his poncho up around his knees and felt very sorry for himself. Suddenly he heard several small humming sounds coming from up the valley. He looked up and saw in the moonlight a little white shape with long spindly legs picking its way through the small bushes. 'Sumaq!' he cried and jumped up and ran to his little alpaca and gave her a big hug. She was also very happy to see her Boy and nuzzled her head into his chest with a soft hum.

It was getting cold, but Antonio had found his little alpaca and was no longer afraid. He gathered up several armfuls of the dried grasses around them and made a small bed in the shelter of a large rock. He led Sumaq to the shelter and gathered her legs so that she lay down on the grass. Antonio sat down against her warm fur and spread his poncho over his body and her feet. 'Time to sleep now, Sumaq.' he said, and the little alpaca tucked her long neck and face into her Boy's chest and was happy.

It seemed only like a short time, but they had been sleeping for many hours when the first warm rays of Inti came up over the distant mountains down the valley and woke Antonio up. Sumaq was standing nearby eating some grass. Antonio was cold in the morning air and his body was very stiff from lying on the thin bed of grass, but he was happy to see Sumaq.

Sumaq saw that her Boy was awake and gave a little snort. She walked off down the ridge a little distance and turned and looked at Antonio as if to say, 'come on, this the way home!' Antonio went to her, and she moved off again, turned her heard and snorted. Antonio knew then that Sumaq knew where she was going so, he followed her down the ridge, though the many small boulders and bushes and across the small patch of snow. After a short time, Sumaq had found the track which led down the valley and so they were able to walk with more confidence.

The light was getting brighter now and in the far distance Antonio could see a lone figure walking up the track to meet them. It was Papa Alberto. Antonio was frightened. What would his Papa do because he had disobeyed and had run off?" The old priest looked around at the children with a grim face.

"He will get a hiding!" stated Andrés with some authority.

"He will give his little boy a big hug because he has found him safe and well." said Mariangeles with more compassion.

"Yes, my child." Padre Pablo beamed at the little girl. "That is exactly what he did…in fact he ran up the track to meet his son and threw his arms around him and gave him a big hug. 'I have found you at last.' Papa Alberto said with tears in his eyes. 'And you have found your little alpaca!' He said, giving Sumaq a pat on her head. 'But you were wrong to have gone searching by yourself. Next time we all look together and little Sumaq should not be allowed to go up into the dangerous mountains by herself.'

With that, Papa Alberto patted Sumaq to go on down the track before them and he took Antonio's hand and they both walked together. 'Abuelo Tomás will be worried about us but he will have some hot mate[24] and cakes.'

And so, they went back down the mountain with the morning light of Inti smiling upon them; the little lost alpaca who had found that she was happy to be what she was, and not something which she could not be, and the little

[24] *Tea. Mate de coca is tea made from coca leaves and is good for extra energy and altitude sickness.*

boy who had found his alpaca and had had his
first night in the mountains alone."

Story Two

The Little Gaucho
(El Pequeño Gaucho)

This is a story from Argentina; that turbulent land of vast plains called the Pampas, the tango and of cowboys known as Gauchos. It is a true story, so I am told. And if you should wander into some small village in Argentina, you may find a small shrine and in it a figure of a small gaucho; the Robin Hood of Argentina.

The two men sat in the ruins of what had been a fine house in the barrio of Mataderos, in the south-west end of the city of Buenos Aires, Argentina. Perhaps the name of the neighbourhood was prophetic as it means "slaughterhouse" in Spanish, for this is where much of the cattle from the Argentine Pampas were processed. There had been another form of slaughtering here on that day of the 21st of June in 1880 when the final battle of the Argentinian Revolution of 1880 had been fought between the

Province of Buenos Aires and the National government. Antonio Tejedor, the Governor of Buenos Aires Province had attempted to stop the federation of his city into the national government and had declared Buenos Aires as independent from the Argentine republic. Subsequently, a brief but bloody war was fought when troops of the national army entered the city.

The two men were soldiers; one an English Colonel who had seen too much of war in other countries and had newly been appointed as an advisor to the National Army only to find himself in the middle of a brief but bloody war. The other man was a young Lieutenant of the National Army who was newly indoctrinated into the horrors of war. Both men were covered in the dirt and blood of the battle which had raged in what had been a beautiful city. But now the war was over, and the city was now at peace under the National Government.

The Colonel looked down at the dusty debris which would have once been a fine, tiled portico and made a circle in the dirt with his sword. He spat into its centre and looked up at his young companion. "You know Teniente[25], wars are a curse upon Mankind. They are started by greedy politicians and finished by soldiers like us. In the middle, many poor, innocent civilians die. For what? So, they can have control over one place of another until some other politician decides otherwise." He hung his head down between his knees and sobbed. He had fought in many wars but his unwilling involvement in this short struggle for political power was the biggest disgrace of his career. "What is there now in life for us?"

The young Lieutenant still retained much of the optimism of youth and saw that the city as being liberated and united with the rest of the country.

"It will be alright now mi Colonel." He said, putting his arm across the shoulders of the older

[25] *Lieutenant*

man. "Here! Let me tell you a story which may give you some hope." So, this is his story:

"I was brought up at the English Mission at Ushuaia at the very end of our country. At the Mission, Dona Maria our teacher would tell us all sorts of wondrous tales about the mountains and the people of the Pampas[26]. Especially stories about the wild gauchos. Do you know about the gauchos, Colonel?"

"No." he replied. "I have heard of them, of course but know very little about them. They are like the North American cowboys I believe?"

"Oh, no, Señor". He replied. "They are much more colourful and romantic than the cowboys of the North Americans. There they are mere vaqueros,[27] but a gaucho is a skilled horseman, brave, unruly and always a colourful character.

[26] *From the Quechua 'pampa', meaning "plain" are the fertile South American grassy lowlands which cover much of southern Argentina.*
[27] *The term 'vaquero' is derived from the Spanish word from 'vaca', meaning 'cow and are mounted cow herders.*

They are a national symbol and are greatly admired and renowned for their deeds. They are not mere herders of cattle, even if that is their main occupation." The young man smiled with some personal pride "Would you like to hear about one of our most famous gauchos? It is a most interesting story, especially for an educated man like yourself."

"Ah, you flatter me, Teniente." The Colonel laughed. "But yes, I would very much like to hear your story. Please go on."

"Well then!" He said. "Listen to this story for it has romance, adventure and faith, all mixed together! This story was told to us at the Mission by Dona Maria, our teacher who had arrived in Ushuaia only a few years before my family arrived. Of course, you know of your own legend of Robin Hood?"

"Indeed, I do" The Colonel replied smiling.

"Well then this is about the 'Robin Hood' of Argentina but unlike the English story, this is the true story of Gauchito[28] Gil, a legendary character of Argentina who is regarded as the most prominent folk hero in our country. Father also knew of him, for the gaucho was born near Mercedes, a town just to the west of Buenos Aires where my family also came from. Because of this, he was able to tell me some of Gauchito Gil's history not known by many. It was a very popular story whilst Gil lived and it became more exciting after he died, which was only two years before we came to Ushuaia. His life was happening when I was a boy in Mercedes, but it was not as popular there as in the countryside, because we saw Buenos Aires as our main city and it was an independent city, often argued over by the large landowners and caudillos[29].

[28] *"Little Gaucho"*

[29] *Generally meaning a strong leader who exercised military power. There were many such caudillos in Argentina in the 19th century who were often owners of large estancias or regions and who often fought with the national government.*

Besides, I had other interests as a small boy and any such stories passed through my brain very quickly. It was not until we moved to Ushuaia that Dona Maria's stories of the gauchito's romantic life found a place in my heart. She said that he was the embodiment of many of the best virtues such as charity, brotherly love, obedience to a higher moral standard, defence of outcasts and the poor and of course defiance of corrupt authority. Father, being a soldier was well-acquainted with the more detailed facts of Gauchito Gil's life. Well, to the story!

It is said that he was born in Pay, Ubre, which is near what is now the town of Mercedes in Corrientes Province just west of Buenos Aires, somewhere about 1840 as Antonio Gil Núñez and that he was a typical gaucho. Dona Maria had read many stories in the newspapers about him and described him as being a small, stocky man with long black hair and broad mustachios. He wore a loose pale-blue shirt, often rolled up past his elbows with a red bandana,[30] and long, cream-coloured accordion-pleated trousers, called bombachas de campo, which are buttoned at the ankles and cover the tops of his high leather boots. Around his waist he wore a chiripa, a woollen poncho often fastened between his legs and held by a red sash around his waist. In cold weather, this could also be worn as a true poncho covering his upper body. He also carried the lasso, as well as a long knife in a silver scabbard kept in his sash behind his back. He also carried the boleadoras. Some people call these 'bolas', which are made of leather cords separated to hold three iron balls or stones at their ends. This can be thrown at the legs of an animal to entwine and immobilize it. He must have cut a gallant figure, but then that is the style of the gaucho!

Estrella Díaz de Miraflores, so the story goes, was a widow and the wealthy owner of the

---

[30] *Large neckerchief of red cotton folded into a triangle and worn around the neck or over the face in dust clouds.*

estancia upon which Gil worked. It was said that the dashing gaucho fell in love, but her brothers thought that it was very improper for a woman of wealth and fine breeding to sully herself with a gaucho. Indeed, it certainly riled the local police commissioner, who himself had eyes for the widow. He conspired with Doña Estrella's brothers to frame Gil for robbery and get rid of him. Hearing of this plot, Gil fled the estancia and joined the army.

Now at that time in 1864, the political climate of the region was extremely volatile. It was also the year in which I was born. There had been some dispute between Paraguay and Brazil which had also helped to change the government in Uruguay. The dictator of Paraguay, Francisco Solano López, feeling that his position was threatened, declared war on Brazil. López's action was viewed by many as aggression for self and national aggrandizement as he had the largest army in all of South America. To counter this aggression, the president of Argentina, Bartolomé Mitre made an alliance with the new government of Uruguay and joined Brazil against Paraguay. This was called the War of the Triple Alliance. This may seem a bad move by the three countries of the alliance all of which had been involved in other wars just prior to this. And don't forget that Paraguay under their aggressive dictator López had a very large army and wished to expand his territories. Independently all prepared for war, Argentina, Brazil, and Uruguay were able to stop Paraguay's powerful military's early advances and in time were able to defeat Paraguay by their combined efforts. By the time the war was over, more than half of the population of Paraguay had perished, including most of its young men making it proportionally the most horrendous and destructive war in South American history.

It was into this war that Gauchito Gil ventured. Naturally he joined the Argentinian Cavalry where his skills as a horseman were much favoured. He was in the forces which repulsed the invasion of Argentina's northern province of Correntes, and then at the bloody battle of Tuyutí, which is in Paraguay just over the border, about a year later. My father was also at this battle. He was only a Capitán then, but he and his engineers were charged with building a temporary road through the marshes and lagoons in front of the Paraguayan defences - the word 'Tuyutí, means 'white mud' in the language of the local Guarani people. Here he witnessed the charges of our cavalry of which Trooper Gil was undoubtedly a member. He said that their charges were magnificent. The Paraguayan infantry was on the high ground beyond the marshes and our cavalry swept up the ridge towards them. Their sabres flashed in the sunlight. The sounds of the hooves of their horses sounded like thunder across the hills. The line of infantry ran to form a defensive square and then the horsemen were upon them. The volleys of the infantry felled many a horse and rider and the sound of sabre upon bayonet rang down to my father who saw it all. One horseman was able to jump over the line and into the square but was dragged from his horse and bayoneted. After a brief struggle the line held, and our gallant horsemen were forced to withdraw. They regrouped and charged again. Again, they were repulsed. Again, they charged and again they were forced to withdraw with heavy losses. The Paraguayans too, had suffered. The ranks of their square were cut in many places. Dead and dying men and horses lay in small heaps across the hill. The infantry clustered together and then were formed back into line by those officers who had survived the charges. The remains of our cavalry were driven off by a regiment of cavalry from the Paraguayan lines. It was a day of slaughter, my father said. Afterward, my father said that the Paraguayans lost over thirteen thousand men killed or captured and our losses were only several hundred. That was dreadful carnage. War cannot be described in terms of the numbers of casualties only, for there are many who also suffered who are not listed as casualties of war.

Gil was one of these. He had received only minor wounds in his charges against the Paraguayans, but he had been horrified by the great slaughter which he had witnessed. He had seen the futility of war with the suffering and disgust which was hidden by their initial euphoric feelings of honour and glory. With the war over, he returned to his home in Corrientes Province. Here he was treated as a hero of the war by the local people for he preached peace and the brotherhood of Mankind. Unfortunately, this was not a time of peace in Argentina. Civil war had again broken out between the moderate Colorado Party and the Celestes, those who wished for a unified government based in Buenos Aires. When Gil tried to return to his village, he was captured and made to enlist to fight against the Colorado Party. He had had enough of war. He appealed to his captors to relent and make peace with their fellow Argentinians. For this he was considered a deserter, and a coward but he was taken never-the-less.

Now here is where the legend of Gauchito Gil starts! No one can say for sure what happened next. Some say that Gil and the other 'volunteers', were locked up in a storehouse whilst the recruiting team went to a nearby cantina for wine. Gil often carried a knife in his boot, and it is possible that he used this to free the lock of the storehouse so that he and his companions could escape. When they did so, most ran off to go to their homes and family but two, also gauchos, stayed with Gil to steal the horses of the recruiters to gallop off into the pampas.

Here they soon gathered like-minded men, and some women, who had been driven away from their homes by the warring factions looking for recruits or plunder. Some fled oppression by wealthy estancieros,[31] while others simply wanted a life of adventure. Whatever their reason, they were attracted to the doctrines of peace and companionship offered by Gil in a time of civil war and self-protection. Out on the pampas, the group were safe. They knew the local land well and sometimes had the protection of the local gauchos who saw them as their own people. Whenever they found someone deserving their help, they would steal cattle from an estancia or raid a storehouse to give to the oppressed. Gil became adored by the poor people of the pampas who saw him as an honest thief with a kind heart who advocated peace and love for all, especially those in need.

Of course, in such volatile times, such ideals could not be tolerated by the authorities, so they became determined to hunt him down. There are many versions of the story of Gil's capture and death. One says that he was captured whilst

[31] *Owners of the estancias or cattle ranches who were often a law unto themselves.*

at a fiesta to honour St Baltasar where he was betrayed by a friend, but I find that difficult to believe considering the love that the people had for Gil. Others say that he was ambushed by the authorities on his way to the fiesta at Mercedes, and this is the story which I would like to believe. Anyway, he was taken.

What happened next is also open to question but, the end result was the same. He was to be taken to the courthouse at the town of Goya which is about fifty kilometres west of Mercedes. Along the way he was murdered. Some say that he was shot by the troops whilst trying to escape. This would be a weak ending for such a man. Several myths say that the Sargento of the troop hated Gil. Perhaps the Sargento was related to those of Gil's past, the brothers of Dona Estrella. Who can tell? It is said that they hung the poor gauchito upside down from a carob tree like they do to beasts which they have slaughtered. Some say they did this to avoid his gaze when they cut his throat. Whichever was the form of his death, one part of the story always comes out. It is always said that before his death, the gauchito told his executioner that he was a man free of sin and that he would forgive him. Furthermore, he said that the Sargento's son lay at home dying and that once in Heaven he would intercede on his behalf. The Sargento, a tough veteran of many wars scoffed at this and slit Gil's throat.

Having done his duty and rid the world of the thief Gil, the Sargento continued with his men to Goya. When he arrived, he found that Gaucho Gil had been pardoned of his crimes and would have been freed had he not been executed. The Sargento went to his house and found that his son was indeed on the brink of death. He prayed to Gaucho Gil for aid, and soon as if by a miracle, his son fully recovered. This filled him with much remorse both in being overzealous and killing an innocent man as well as disbelieving Gil's prophesy. In shame and in appreciation for what he believed the spirit of Gil had done, the Sargento went back to the site of the murder and found that the body had been removed for burial. He erected a cross in the ground that had been reddened by Gaucho Gil's blood and later returned with a small statue made in Gil's likeness – a gaucho in a blue shirt and cream trousers, red neckerchief and holding his bolos in his right hand. He placed this statue in front of the cross and the devotion to Gaucho Gil began. Who knows? Perhaps one day he may be made a saint.

Well, Señor Colonel, did you like my stories from the county of my birth?"

"I did. And I am also glad that we have had the opportunity to talk in such an amenable manner. For in some little way, you have also restored my faith in the goodness of humankind."

The two men rose and walked off down the wide avenue towards the centre of the city and both hoped that one day, it would again regain its splendour.

Story Three

The Shoeshine Boy of La Paz
(El Lustrabotas de La Paz)

Another true story based upon my own encounter with the Shoeshine Boys of La Paz, the biggest city in Bolivia. It is a story about the value of honest work and how even a small act can bring much satisfaction.

It was after dinner, a few nights ago, when my employer, Don Emiliano and I had retired from the table after an excellent meal. Young Marcus, my partner's apprentice and the only other employee from our mining company staying at the hotel in Potosi, had left as was his usual custom.

As we settled down in the large armchairs in front of the fire, for it was becoming cold at night, Don Emiliano poured out a generous glass of a fine Colheita[1], and leaned over towards me.

"You know, Ernesto," he said, raising the glass to look at the clarity of the wine, "I am sometimes worried about that young man. He is a good administrator and comes from a fine family, but he is not happy here."

"He seems to carry himself well and is quite respectful to me. The men at the mine seem to respect him also." I remarked.

"Yes, that is true." Don Emiliano continued. "He is generally very thorough for such a young man, but I feel that he thinks that being a junior supply officer in our company is below his station. He is of mixed birth, but his father is a well-respected in the export business and a with a good reputation as an honest hard worker, who was trustworthy when it comes to doing business."

[1] *Pronounced [col-ay-ta], is a tawny port from a single vintage aged for at least seven years in the barrel.*

"Ah! I understand the young man's problem" I commented." He is like many young men of this generation. He wants everything at once and has too much pride to want to start at the bottom and work for the exalted status which is assumed owed is to him."

"Oh yes, Ernesto" he replied." It seems to be the expectation of our young people to want now what their parents took years to gain through hard work."

I was probably due to the good wine and the comfort of our hotel room, so I recounted an episode of my early life to illustrate my thoughts. "I have found, Don Emiliano, that it is not the work that a person does which is the true value of their life, but how they perform that work. Luckily, I found this truth when I was still a young man. May I be permitted to tell you, my story?"

"I would be honoured, Señor, if you would." said my employer refilling my empty glass with another generous measure of his fine port.

I continued with my story.

"A very long time ago; too long for me to mention in years, I too was a young man with all of the pride and thoughts of future grandeur which no doubt resides in the mind of our young Marcus. Although I was raised and lived in Copacabana, my employer had requested that I accompany him and another senior official to a conference in the Bolivian capital of La Paz. I suspect that my father's political connections had something to do with this. Have you been to La Paz, Don Emiliano?"

"Ah yes!' he replied with a broad smile "The beautiful city of Nuestra Señora de La Paz[2]. I have been there once, but it was too high and enclosed for my liking. Remember that I was raised on the coast until it was taken away by the Chileans."

[2] *In English, "Our Lady of the Peace" is the full name of this city, still the most well-known city in Bolivia and site of many of its financial institutions, although Santa Cruz de la Sierra is now the biggest city and Sucre is its capital.*

"Oh!" I replied in mock horror. "You do not like our mountains! Yes, La Paz is a beautiful city and being set at the bottom of a long, deep canyon surrounded by mountains and the altiplano, it can be a daunting place. Especially if there are earth tremors which are common enough there.

Copacabana on Lago Titicaca is a very significant religious site of the early Aymara people who have lived there for centuries and later of the Incas who adopted this Aymara veneration. Its name of the town is thought to have come from the Aymara 'kota Kawana,' meaning 'a view of the lake',[3] and on one side of the small but pleasant Plaza de Armes, are the impressive white buildings of the Basilica of Our Lady of Copacabana. It is interesting to note that our neighbours in Brazil have given a beach in their city of Rio de Janeiro the very same name of Copacabana. One may think that an Amaya-speaking wit has passed a sarcastic

[3] *There is also a suggestion that it may have been derived from 'Kotakawana, a god of fertility in ancient Andean mythology,*

comment on the peaceful nature of the mighty Atlantic Ocean there, but that is unlikely considering the Ocean's storms. No, the real reason of why an Aymara term should be given to a Brazilian beach is that more recently a chapel was built there to hold a replica of the same statue of Our Lady of Copacabana which resides in the Basilica of our Bolivian town.

The next morning our coach set off early, climbing slowly up into the hills which surround Copacabana. The road was good, but wound tightly from one hilltop to the next, mostly with glorious views of the lake behind us. These hills were mainly devoid of trees, but the pasture was green with a few small streams running down towards the lake. Across the hills cut several sharp spines of rock which had been upturned by some great upheaval in the distant past.

A few hours later, we descended into the little town of San Pedro de Tiquina, situated on a narrow strip of land opposite a broad strait of water. It was here that Lake Titicaca narrowed down to about five hundred metres. On a good map, this strait formed the neck of the puma which the Old People likened to the shape of the Lake. Further to the south, the lake opened up again to form the head of the puma. Here we were requested to alight and make our way to the waterfront where a boatman ushered us into his small craft, and for a few coins took us across the water to San Pablo de Tiquina on the opposite shore. Meanwhile, our coach with its four horses still in harness, and all of our luggage, was carefully taken on board a low punt made of large logs lashed together. Only the two boatmen were permitted on board this craft which was then slowly poled over to the San Pablo side.

After some refreshment at a small cantina facing the main plaza of the town, we again joined our coach for the last leg of our journey to La Paz. This was uneventful and was along a small section of the altiplano above the hills south of the lake with the line of snow-capped mountains to our east. It was near nightfall when our coach came to the staging post at El

Alto[4]. There were a few small buildings, badly constructed, which housed the people who looked after the coach and horses and provided some poor accommodation for travellers such as us. Below us in a long valley stretching a long way further south were the myriad lights of the city of Nuestra Señora de La Paz over a thousand metres below us. As the road down the narrow ravine into the city was both steep and narrow, we were obliged to stay the night at El Alto.

It was still dark; just before dawn and the rays of the sun were just backlighting the snows on the peaks to the east. This morning, the ostler[5] had replaced our horses with four strong mules which would be better in handling the coach down the steep declines. We set off full of trepidation, but the mules were sturdy and the

[4] *Meaning "The Halt" in Spanish and was the stopping place of the conquistador Alonso de Mendoza (1471-1549) the founder of the city of Nuestra Señora de La Paz in 1548. Since then, El Alto has grown to be the second biggest city of Bolivia.*
[5] *The ostler is the person who looks after horses and hitches up the team to a coach.*

two coachmen skilled in handling the brake. Soon we were at the end of the ravine and happily jangling down the narrow, cobbled streets of La Paz. On the avenida Illampu we stopped at a fashionable hotel built in the European style where we were to spend the night. The porter having taken our bags to our rooms and the manager having given us our keys, my enthusiasm for this new city was too much, so I bade farewell to my colleagues and went for a short walk down the avenue.

The first street which I encountered was called calle[6] Santa Cruz, which ran steeply downhill to the left. It seemed to have some promise as it contained several small shops selling a variety of foods. Further down the street, the shops seemed to take on a religious tone with names such as 'Chifleria[7] of the Angels,' and 'Market of the Spirits'. On closer inspection, I found that the many items which were on display were all of those items which were needed for the old

---

[6] *Street*
[7] *A booth or small shop*

religion. There was a great variety of painted clay statues of the many Andean deities, bags of sweet-smelling herbs and dried llama foetuses hanging from their awnings. Suddenly I recalled what I had read about La Paz. This was the famous El Mercado de las Brujas or the 'Witches Market' where practitioners of the old religion could buy what was necessary to obtain the help of the ancient deities. Here one could buy medicinal herbs for one's ailments, or have their fortune read in leaves of the coca plant, or buy the llama foetus which would be burnt at the beginning of a prayer to Pachamama, the earth goddess, so that one could receive health and prosperity for some future undertaking.

I was not horrified at these items. To be sure, some of the dried llamas, toads and other unrecognisable animal bodies were unpleasant to an educated eye with a Christian upbringing, but this is part of the wide Andean culture and has been practiced well before the Holy Fathers brought Christianity to the mountains. From my own family experience, I have witnessed my uncles performing such rituals for various requests, and then go to mass and pray to Our Lady for the same thing. There seems to be a blurring of thought when it comes to Our Lady and Pachamama. Who am I to judge? It is, after all a matter of faith. But one thing is certain in the mountains; this faith is strong and guides the people in their daily tasks and they seem to be better than those whom I have met in the lowland cities whose faith seems to be somewhat narrower and less sincere.

But now, Don Emiliano, you may be wondering about this journey and el lustrabota? Well, the journey from Copacabana to La Paz was very exciting for a young man such as I and worth telling as it now leads up to my philosophical view about the ethics of honest work."

Don Emiliano lent across the table to light his cigar. "No, please go on. Your travels interest me a great deal. I myself, have never been to that region and being lowland bred have only the local stories now to help me think how the true Andino lives."

"Thank you, Don Emiliano. Then I will conclude my story: continuing my walk down the street of the brujas with its many shops with herbs, statues and masks, I noticed a thin young man who wore a bandana around his face. He was sitting on a small wooden box and was offering to clean the shoes of all who passed. I had remembered seeing similar men as we passed the many small plazas as we came into the city. These were the local shoeshine boys who, for a few small coins would give your boots a quick shine and then scurry off to seek a new location. They hid their faces in their bandanas because they were ashamed of their lowly work. The masks and bandanas they wore were to protect their identity. What shame would it be for a hard-working family who had moved off their poor farms into the city to have their young men work as servants, cleaning the boots of strangers? Also, these men were proud. Why would a young Señorita[8] be attracted to a lowly shoeshine boy?

[8] *Young lady "Miss"*

I quickly passed him by. It was not because my boots did not need a shine. Far from it! The long journey had dulled their appearance, and as a young clerk of the lowest rank I had no-one to polish my boots for me, and perhaps I too, was ashamed of my appearance. Or perhaps I did not want to join in the young man's self-pity, and use his time to perform this lowly function. I cannot recall, but I passed on down the cobbled street to where it opened out into a very large plaza. This was the Park Major also known as the Square of Saint Francis. On the corner and around to my right were several small tables with street vendors selling small trinkets and sweets. In front at some distance was the bustling avenida Mariscal Santa Cruz[9].

I turned the corner and walked into the plaza. Downhill, at its far end, was the Basilica of San Francisco, an imposing building made from yellow stone with a single large bell tower. I went in and lit a candle in thanks for our safe journey – or perhaps as a confirmation of my

---

[9] *Marshal Santa Cruz Avenue*

faith after having passed through the Witches Market. A passing official of the church stopped and offered me his greeting. We fell into conversation, for he was proud of his church. He told me that the Franciscans had been in this area before the city was founded by the conquistador Alonso de Mendoza in 1548. Their leader, Fray Francisco de Morales had been welcomed and given land by the chief of the local Aymara people. This is where a small church was built here on the banks of the Choqueyapu River. No doubt the local people were impressed by the poverty and humility of the Franciscan friars. When Don Alonzo arrived, a more substantial church was built but its roof collapsed after a heavy snowfall in 1612.

In such a remote locality with more pressing matters to attend to, the church stood unfinished for over a century. Eventually construction recommenced allowing this fine building to be completed in 1758. It was named in honour of its founder, Fray Francisco de los Angeles Morales, whose remains are entombed in the church. The Sacristan, for that was the title of my new friend, took me for a walk around the magnificent interior, then up a very narrow flight of stairs to the first storey of the imposing bell tower, which was completed in 1885. Here was a wide vista of the city which sloped away down the long valley to the south and into the centre of commerce with its European buildings made of fine stone. In the distance were the snow-capped peaks of La Paz's dominant mountain, Illimani. This name comes from an Aymara word meaning 'water bearer', it is considered the queen of the mountain deities within Bolivia.

After my tour of the Basilica, I exited the beautifully ornate doors out into the plaza which bears the same name. I had walked only a few paces when I was struck by the sight of a rather ornate chair nestling under the trees to one side of the plaza. Here was another shoeshine stand, but one with a great difference. Here was no simple wooden box upon which el lustrabota kept his few meagre tools, and then used it as a footrest for his customers. Here was a proud, upright chair of substantial proportions and comfort. It even had a small canopy which jutted out over the head of the customer to afford some protection from the sun. The shoeshine boy was also different. To use the term 'boy' would be an insult. This man was of about middle age and unlike his younger competitors, wore no mask to hide his face which had been darkened and lined with many years out in the elements.

Now, my boots were black riding boots, typical of a travelling young man, and they had had much neglect over the last few days. Even in the home, a young man must clean his own boots, and rarely has the services of a servant to perform this duty for him. I waited until the shoe shiner had finished with his last customer, then I walked over and sat down with a cheerful, '¡buenos días! Señor'. He returned my morning salutation with a smile, and he beckoned me to be seated. I then noticed that my boots rested upon a small dais upon which was proudly printed the man's name, Ignacio.

'It is a fine day, Ignacio'. I said.

'Si, Señor. Fine enough for some nice shiny boots.' He laughed.

With that he began his art; for I soon found that he applied his trade with the skill, perfection and care of an artisan. This was no mere lustrabota who quickly gave one's shoes a cursory shine and then took your money. This man loved his work and took professional pride in every action.

First, he brushed over my boots with a fine horse-hair brush to remove the surface dust. It had a finely carved handle of some Andean design. Next, he gently rubbed over the boots with a soft, damp cloth to continue the removal of any dust. He then exchanged this cloth for another and, dipping it into a tin of a creamy mixture he then continued the cleaning process. He wiped this off using a slow circular motion using another, moistened cloth. After the boots had been thoroughly cleaned, he then applied another soft paste which was probably a leather restorer. This he also rubbed in with a slow, circular motion.

These were not his only actions. During this initial cleaning procedure, he had a number of visitors, who would drop a few coins into an ornate wooden box by his side from which Ignacio would extract a broad ticket. This must be a lottery of a kind common to these parts. These acts were usually accompanied by the usual morning salutations; '¡buenos días! Ignacio' most would say because it was obvious that this lustrabota was a well-known and popular figure in the Plaza de San Francisco.

For my part it was also relaxing to sit in this big, comfortable chair whilst my boots were receiving such careful treatment. I had the time to sit back and watch the passing activities in the plaza and on the busy avenue beyond. Here were the usual passing parade of people going about their business: the office workers in their faded dark suits; the ladies in their bright village dresses selling a variety of foods and trinkets, from their stalls which lined one side of the plaza; and the carriages, hand-carts and mounted citizens moving up and down the broad avenida Mariscal Santa Cruz.

Ignacio continued his ministrations with the application of a lustrous black polish which he kept in another can which he had carefully opened. He used a small, circular brush which also had the same motifs carved on its handle. He rubbed in the polish with a soft circular motion, making sure that it penetrated all of the creases of the leather and grooves around the edge of the sole. Then he gave the entire surface of both boots a vigorous lathing, with a soft leather cloth. This was the most extensive part of the treatment and was followed up with more polishing with a hand glove which looked like alpaca wool. Finally, he polished the rims of the sole of the boot with protective oil.

I was amazed at both his care and rapid dexterity. This man had practiced his art over many years and was proud of his work. It was also clear that the local community also shared in his pride and passion, for I had noticed that several other men waited under the trees ready to enjoy the craftsman's skills.

Well! There you have it, Don Emiliano. The story of the lustrabota of La Paz. Perhaps you may be able to gently remind the young Marcus, that it is not the type of work that matters but how it is done that shows the worth of a person.

Also, as my acquaintance with the good Ignacio taught me, the true professional is also usually happy in themselves for doing such a professional job."

The old man smiled and leaned back in his chair and took a long draw on his cigar. "Perhaps you are right Ernesto. Perhaps you are right."

Story Four

Mountains and Mermaids
(Montañas y Sirenas)

This story is from the rich mythology of South America; in this case about the alluring mermaids or Sirenas who inhabit the lakes and deep waterways of the high Andes of Peru and of the lowlands of Amazonia.

The coach was on its long, dusty road south from the city of Cuzco in Peru bound for Puno on Lake Titicaca. A short distance down the road, and coming up the village of Huarcapay, it passed an immense area of wetlands and lagoons consisting of a large lake edged by totora reeds[10]; a flock of white Ibis took flight from its foreshore as the coach rattled past.

---

[10] *Totora reeds -* **Schoenoplectus californicus** *subsp.* **tatora** *is a subspecies of the giant bulrush found in South America, notably on Lake Titicaca and other parts.*

One of the passengers, a rather plump merchant by the look of his well-cut but faded jacket, leaned across to the lady opposite and said in a quiet and almost secretive voice "That is Lake Huarcapay, you see out there, Señora." Regaining his original posture and nodding with his head to the passing vista. "It is noted for its wildlife but there is a darker side to its beauty." He continued. The lady opposite, a thin, scholarly looking woman looked up at him surprise and so he continued. "Some of the locals claim that the lake is a place of dread. They say that people who have ventured out onto the water have often not returned, and that the lake is inhabited by Umantuus and other monsters who come out at night."

"Umantuus?" the lady said in a startled voice "What are they, pray tell, kind sir?" Her voice showed that her Spanish was adequate but not her first language as she was an English tutor travelling to take up a post with a wealthy family in Puno.

"Yes. What our European ancestors would call 'mermaids'. They have the usual body of a man or woman but the hind section of a fish. However, our local mermaids are of the freshwater variety and inhabit only lakes and streams; they are not the Pincoy who are their cousins and who live in the seas. They are sometimes called 'sirena' as in the sirens of ancient Greece and in the province of Lampa, not far from Puno, close to Lake Titicaca, there are several places named 'Sirenayoc' which combines this Spanish word 'sirena' and the Quechua word 'yoc' for 'who owns', so the total meaning is 'where there are mermaids'. In Chile, they are also called 'Coñi Lafquen' or Lake Maidens and are said to have long, golden hair which they brush in the moonlight and are said to lure unsuspecting young fishermen from their reed boats. They are said to also inhabit Lake Titicaca and are the servants of the god who lives under the water."

"'Kotakawana' he is called." The man sitting next to the lady replied with some authority.

"Ah! I see you know something of our legends here in the south." The merchant exclaimed with a smile across his thin lips.

"My studies in philosophy have had such directions at the university in Cuzco where I teach, and the belief of the ancients is a fascinating subject in its own right." The man replied.

"That is very true, Señor." replied the merchant. "Whilst my ancestry is partly European and I am a true man of God, I have found that there is room in our theology for the beliefs of the local people. You will even see our mermaids carved on the façade of the cathedral at Puno in the Plaza de Armas[11]. The people may come to our churches to say Mass, but they will still burn a llama foetus as a sacrifice to the apu[12] of the

[11] *The Plaza de Armas ("Arms Square") is the major plaza in the city, similar to other South American cities. On some recent maps it is called the Plaza Mayor de Puno ("Main Square of Puno")*
[12] *Apu – the god attributed to particular mountains in the high Andes.*

mountain before taking their herds to its summer pastures."

"Yes! That is very important to these simple people who have been able to accommodate the old beliefs into Christianity, so who are we to put them to ridicule?" the philosopher replied with a faint smile.

"Again, that is also true. You are indeed a true philosopher, but I suspect that you know more about the common people than a cloistered academic! You have the height and thin face of a European but the high cheekbones of the Andino, Señor Santiago here," the merchant turned to the small man sitting next to him and who had been noticeably quite during the trip, "if I may continue my humble observations, Santiago is my servant and a true Andino – a man of these mountains." He continued with an enigmatic smile and sideways glance at his servant.

"You are very perceptive, Señor," The philosopher replied, "as you have deduced, I am a mestizo and my mother's family can be traced back to Incan nobility. And I am sure that Señor Santiago, here is of the Quechua-speaking people who have long lived in these mountains of Peru."

"That is true, Señor." said Santiago with a huge grin; no longer the humble manservant but now a fellow traveller.

"Imanallatac canqui?[13]" asked the philosopher in Quechua.

"Allillanmi[14]" Santiago replied without thinking, using the Runasimi or Cuzco dialect of Quechua, then looked at his employer with some apprehension.

[13] *Imanallatac canqui? ("EE-mah-nah-YA-tahk CAHNG-ee.") Quechua for a generalised term of informal greeting loosely translated to "How are you" but showing some pleasure in the meeting.*
[14] *Allillanmi (AYI -yanmi) – "I'm fine." in Quechua.*

"Ah! I see that you have the Quechua language, a northern dialect, perhaps from Ecuador, Señor Santiago", the philosopher replied smiling.

"You are a man of constant surprises, Señor, "the merchant said with a smile. You are indeed a scholar as you also have the Runasimi[15] of the Old People[16]."

The conversation continued for some time between the merchant and the philosopher about the current use of the old Incan language of Quechua in many countries of the Andes, where the old Incan Empire had spread. It was almost nightfall as the coach crossed the small stone bridge over the river and rattled into the small hamlet of Huarcapay and the stop for the night.

[15] *How the Quechua-speaking peoples referred to their language.*
[16] *Used here, 'Old People' refers to the pre-Spanish people of the Andes such as the Inca and the Aymara*

As the coach pulled into the courtyard of the staging post, the merchant again leaned over and said in almost a confidential tone: "Here the Urubamba River is called the Willkanuta which is an Aymara term meaning, 'the house of the Sun,' for this river was sacred to the people and it is also called the 'sacred river,' in the Quechua language"

"Yes," the philosopher replied, "it has many names in many local languages, but it has always been a source of life in these mountains."

"In many ways, Señor." The merchant replied. "There is a nearby peak here which is called 'Quri,' which in the Quechua language means 'gold'; something of which our Spanish ancestors would have had the greatest interest."

Here, the mighty Urubamba River had slowed its mad rush from the snow-capped mountains further north and now flowed lazily along the small plain between the road and the barren hills. Now the valley was covered in deep shadow as the sun had slowly crept below the mountains.

The night at the coaching inn was a comfortable one despite the cold wind which blew down off the snow-capped peaks beyond the hills which surrounded the town. There was a good fire prepared in the inn's front room where the owner welcomed his guests with a substantial Seco Tajime,[17] and freshly baked bread rolls. The evening quickly passed in these comfortable surroundings, with cigars and a little wine after an excellent dinner. Santiago, usually reserved and constantly occupied with the needs of his master, was invited to join the rest of the company in front of the bright crackling fire and by now, he too had relaxed. He spoke of his family and of little farm in the hills above Cuzco where he had been raised as the youngest of a large family. His childhood had been a happy one but alas as he grew to manhood it was soon

[17] *Seco Tajime or Seco de Carne is a typical Peruvian stew of mutton with potatoes, pumpkin, peas, onions with garlic and cilantro (an herb similar to coriander).*

necessary to leave and seek employment in the city.

The lady had remained quiet for most of the conversation; sipping her small glass of wine and listening intently to the conversation between the men. At an early hour, she rose and gave her apologies and went upstairs to her room. Not long afterwards, the philosopher also said "¡buenas noches![18]" and retired as tomorrow would be another long journey. The merchant and his servant, Santiago were left alone to enjoy the comforting cracking fire and the remains of the good wine which the philosopher had bought for the company.

"You know Jefe[19] - ," Santiago said when they were alone and the inn was quiet, "that I came from a small farm near Cuzco. The waters there are thin and narrow with hardly a place for even a fish to live and certainly not a water

[18] *"Good Night"*
[19] *Jeffe (pronounced 'hey-fe') is a familiar term for 'boss' or 'chief'*

spirit like the one which you described earlier. Please. Tell me more about these people who live in that lake outside?"

The merchant smiled and took another sip of his wine, a fine local red variety from a vineyard near Curahuasi,[20] just to the west of Cuzco. "Ah! You ask me of something which I delight in telling. You know that I have travelled around this great continent of ours since I was a young man in my father's business. Being a mestizo, I have always been interested in the customs and stories from my mother's people who have lived in these mountains well before the Spaniards came. But I digress! Yes! The Umantuus. They are said to live in the lakes and larger rivers. They are called other names in other countries. In the jungles of the mighty Amazon River to our east, in both Peru and our neighbours to the north, they are also called the Yacuruna – "

<hr>

[20] *Curahuasi (pronounced 'Cooru –wahsi') is a city about 120 km. west of Cuzco*

"The 'river man' in our Quechua language!" Santiago replied with some joy that he was able to add to the story.

"–yes! That is right, Santiago. But the Yacuruna are said to be hairy with a backward-facing head and deformed feet, not like our lovely maidens, the Umantuus. Although it is also said that these ugly creatures can transform themselves into handsome young men should they find a young girl worthy to be taken as a wife."

Santiago cringed at such a suggestion but relaxed and took up his wine glass to sooth his nerve. Like many poor Andino, he was superstitious and would believe any tale of the supernatural. Even though he attended Mass every Sunday with his family, he knew that it was also the way of his father to burn a llama foetus to honour the Apus or gods of the mountains, before taking their llamas up to the higher pastures. He had even seen Father José, once at a blessing ceremony at a neighbour's farm, throw a little wine on the ground to honour Pachamama, the Earth goddess of the Old People.

The merchant refilled his glass and continued: "Yes, the idea that our deep waters contain spirit people is widespread here in South America, and other countries. In Brazil, that country to the east, where the Amazon River runs, they also have beautiful maidens called the Uauyara, or simply the Yara, who sometimes take fishermen for their husbands. But alas, they are immortal and as their husbands are not, the marriage is doomed from the start. Like our Umantuus, the Uauyara also like to come to the surface on bright moonlit nights and sing alluring melodies to attract foolish young men from the villages."

"Are the Yara truly beautiful and not ugly like the Yacuruna?" Santiago asked with some enthusiasm for he liked hearing tales of beautiful young women.

The merchant looked into the broad, honest face of his servant and smiled. "Oh, they are said by many to be very beautiful. Some stories say that they have long hair, sometimes dark green, at other times very black and even some are said to have blonde hair, white faces and blue eyes like the fair ladies from Europe. Who knows?" He took up the small poker near the fire grate and gave the fire, which had now dwindled down to some small hot coals, a strong prod to spread the coals around the grate. "Well! Santiago my friend, it is time for bed. We have another long day on the road to Puno." He stood up and stretched, took a last swallow of the remains of his wine and left.

Santiago finished his wine and went out of the warm room, and through the front door of the inn as it was the usual custom of such an establishment to accommodate servants outside, in quarters within the barn. Santiago knew from experience that they would generally be more comfortable than the poor bed on which he had slept in his family's farm with his other three brothers; but he would still have to go outside.

It was a lovely, clear night common to this altitude in the high Andes. Mamma Killa[21], brightly shone her large smiling face high in the sky and Santiago could see the rugged hills surrounding the town. He was not tired but could feel the numbing effects of the wine, something that he rarely drank, for chicha, the corn beer brewed by his family and those of many generations before them, was what he usually drank.

The inn was on the edge of town, on the main road which ran between Cuzco in the north to Puno to the south and so Santiago decided that a short walk in the cold air would help to clear his head. He walked down to the edge of the lake and sat down on a small, dusty mound surrounded by clumps of the totora reeds. His mind wandered freely, back to the times of the Old People, his ancestors. Suddenly he could hear a soft, lilting song coming across the water of the lake. He looked out upon its crystal surface, but he could see nothing; perhaps it

[21]*From the Quechua "Mama Killa" for "Mother Moon"*

was only the gentle breeze blowing on his face
after all.

Story Five:

The Salvation of Baños
(La Salvación de Baños)

Baños de Aqua Santa or 'the Baths of the Holy Waters' is a city in the high Andes of Ecuador and sits on the slopes of Tungurahua, *an active volcano. Baños is a spa town with many hot springs and waterfalls; it is also a religious shrine to many Ecuadoreans.*

I had now settled into a comfortable routine at San Rafael, the comfortable hacienda just outside of the town. About seven in the morning, give or take some minutes, as time was not of an importance here, there would be a knock on my door, it would be discretely opened, and Ambrosio, my host's general factotum would enter. Like many of the staff here, he is more like an old friend devoted to his master and of a friendly disposition.

"¡Buenos días! Señor." He would always say, and he would have a hot cup of coffee in one hand and a jug of hot water for my morning ablutions in the other. He would place the jug on the dresser and the cup on my bedside table.

I would thank him, and he would bow and leave, closing the door behind him. After washing and shaving, I would dress ready for breakfast at eight. This was always a punctual time as Don Alejandro, my host, was a fastidious man who kept a regular daily schedule. My clothes from the previous day's travel up the mountains from Quito had been thoroughly cleaned and pressed just after our arrival, but I had also been given a new set of clothing by my host. There is no shortage of necessary items in this old and comfortable hacienda.

Breakfast was taken in the main hall at long table occupied only by Don Alejandro and myself. My servants, as was befitting their rank in this formal setting, ate with the other men of the hacienda in a room next to the kitchen. Coffee and an assortment of bread and pastries with jam and cheese were served, and sometimes Ambrosio would ask if we would like an egg. This was usually lightly fried on one side and served separately on a small plate.

Conversation would usually be minimal although Don Alejandro always acted as a good host and would enquire after my health and apologise for any inconvenience and the lack of entertainment. He had a good supply of old books and was very generous with his wine, spirits and cigars, all of which were of the best quality.

Wiping his chin with his napkin as a sign that he had finished his meal, Don Alejandro looked up and smiled. "It will be a fine day, today my friend. Would you care to ride with me into the town and see some more of our fine country? Perhaps it will not be as exciting as other places which you have visited but certainly of some interest never-the-less"

This a great opportunity to more of this fascinating country, so I readily agreed with my old host and that I would like to see more of his country as I had spent most of my life abroad and in my home country of Peru. So, after we had finished our leisurely breakfast, Don Alejandro had his servants provide me with a fine horse from his small stable. It was still very early in the morning full, of clear mountain air and long shadows as we rode out through the gates of the hacienda at a very relaxed pace.

The road was merely a cart-track which followed the flat, narrow bank of the steep-sided river valley through which the gurgling Pastaza River flows. The hills rose up very high on either side of the valley and unlike those on the western side of the Andes, these slopes were green with lush vegetation. Here and there, where the slope was not severe, some of the natural vegetation had been cleared for small cultivation of crops giving the slopes a patchwork of greens in different shades and textures. To my eye, these crops seem to be hanging onto these slopes with a tenacity only rivalled by the narrow tracks which led up to them.

My host explained that our journey at this leisurely pace would take about three hours, a good time for a discussion away from the life of the hacienda. Mostly we spoke of our personal lives; our homes, our families and of the futility of the conflicts in which our governments seem to entangle themselves.

"You will like our little town of Baños," Don Alejandro said. "It has an interesting history and is one of the places of spiritual significance in our country. Would you like to hear its story?"

"Certainly, Señor," I replied, for I knew that he was both a well-educated man and a good raconteur. So, this is Don Alejandro's story:

"Baños was founded by the Dominicans[1] who set up a small friary in the region around 1570. Of course it had been populated for many years by the Puruhuaes, the local people, who themselves had been assimilated into the Incan Empire in the fifteenth century. No doubt both peoples were attracted to these valleys by the hot springs from the volcano and the fertile soil. For the Incas, this was also a gateway to the Amazon Basin further east, as it still is today. The Inca nobility also liked to come here for bathing in the hot waters which are very beneficial to the health. In the local language of the Puruhuaes they refer to this as 'ishpaypae' –

---

[1] *The Order of Preachers (Latin: Ordo Praedicatorum, O.P.), known as the Dominican Order, is a traveling order of the Roman Catholic Church founded by the Spanish priest Dominic of Caleruega in France in 1216.*

bathing in the urine of Mama Tungurahua[2] – which I do not think was a disrespectful term and is probably best translated in meaning to 'waters'. Certainly, the waters here seem to have a therapeutic value.

So, the Dominicans came and set up their little congregation to bring the word of God to the Heathen. Of course, the local people and their Incan overlords had their own complex religion with Inti the Sun and Pachamama the Earth goddess being most important in their theology. Even today, the people still give offerings to the old deities – just in case - you understand.

One old story recounts how the Sacristan[3] of their church was visited one night by an image of the Virgin Mary who told him that they should build a shrine near one of the many hot springs which occur in the district, and that this

[2]*Pronounced [Tungu-agu-wah] From Quechua tunguri [throat] and rahua [fire] or "throat of fire" is still an active volcano.*
[3] *An official of a church charged with caring for the vessels and other accoutrements of the church*

would be a place of curing and salvation for lepers and others with sickness. So today, in our little stone church we have the statue of Our Lady of the Rosary of Agua Santa de Baños, and our town is a place of pilgrimage from all over the country."

"It makes for a good story, Señor," I commented. "There are many places in my country and in Europe which have special shrines to the Virgin and many of the saints. It builds on the faith of the common people and of course is good revenue for the Church."

"Ah. You are too cynical, Señor." The old man replied. "Many have been cured by these waters. Whether it is by their faith or by the miracles promised by the Virgin, it is beyond the comprehension of a simple man like me.

But there is another legend which concerns the faith of the people of Baños, which perhaps is a lot more dramatic, as it concerns our volcano. Wait and in a few moments when we go around the next corner you will see Mama Tungurahua."

Indeed, as we came around the corner of a steep ridge running down to the river below, I saw at the end of the long, steep-sided valley to our left, the magnificent shape of the volcano Tungurahua.

It had the typical cone shape of Andean volcanoes, similar to others which I had seen in Peru. I found that the Don Alejandro shared my fascination with these giants. Now, sleeping in the distance, it still commanded some degree of awe and inspiration. Its lower slopes were vegetated for the most part except where they had been eroded by landslides. A deep ravine cut into the slope facing us. The summit, now flat and broken by its crater's edge after many eruptions and erosion, was swathed in small white clouds. I had been in one small eruption well to the south in Peru, which had been at a distance, but it was still a terrifying experience. The rapidity of the vertical ejection of a very large cloud of grey ash had been almost unbelievable. The enormous roar of its sound was enhanced by the thunderclaps of the lightning which was generated by such a sudden movement of hot gas and ash. Once the huge mushroom cloud had reached its great height, it spread out on the high altitude winds, and then fell like hot sand upon all in its path. I had felt a little of this hot rain, and had not waited to be overcome. I had spurred my horse to a gallop in a safe direction. And this was considered only a small eruption in an unpopulated region!

Don Alejandro continued his story:

"I think that it was in 1773 when the volcano had a massive eruption or so the Dominican scholar Don Emiliano de Velasco recorded. His description was most horrendous. After days of multiple earth tremors, the volcano belched forth a prodigious amount of ash and heavier material in a great explosion. Luckily most of the fine ash was pushed away from Baños by the prevailing winds which come from the east. This was not good for those in the villages on the other side of the volcano, which were totally destroyed by the ash fall, collapsing buildings and poisoning all of the livestock and crops.

In Baños the population was in a great state of panic but then as the great cloud collapsed, lava and fiery clouds of ash began to flow towards the town over the edge of the crater's rim and down the deep ravine which you can still see on the slopes of this side of the volcano. This is the Quebrada Bascún[4] through which a small stream still runs, right through the western part of the town and into the Rio Pastaza.

Seeing the lava approaching their town, some people ran to the church and brought out the statue of the Virgin de Agua Santa and carried her outside into the plaza, praying to her for their salvation. It is said that someone saw the statue raise its hand and with that the lava stopped at the edge of the town. Another story of the faithful, I suppose, but it is still a good

[4] *Bascún ravine cut by the river of that name.*

story, and I believe that the townspeople plan to rebuild the small stone church as a great basilica for the veneration of our protector, the Virgin de Agua Santa."

It was an interesting story, one which showed the faith of this old man. I have seen many miracles in my lifetime which I cannot explain; mostly the heroic actions of men in difficult situations so I could not comment on Don Alejandro's assessment of the people of Baños. We rode on in silence for a while.

There was a high and cascading waterfall coming down from the rocky cliff on one side of the valley. Don Alejandro pointed up at its waters now shimmering in the noonday sun. "Of course there is also another variation of that story. It is said that an image of the Virgin appeared in one of the many waterfalls which cascade down near the town and that She moved the waters over to fall upon the approaching fiery lava which stopped its progress before reaching the town. Anyway, whatever the version of the story, we believe that Baños was saved by the faith of the people in our protector, Our Lady, the Virgin of Agua Santa."

We rode the short distance remaining down into the steep bank of the Pastaza and up into the town. Here I found streets which were well-paved with cobbles from the stream and small houses made of mudbrick, often limed on the outside and painted in bright colours. The people were obviously proud of their town and seemed happy to see us; many gave personal greetings to my host whose family had lived in the old hacienda for many generations. "Buenas tardes[5], Don Alejandro" they would say with a smile; the men taking off their hats and the ladies giving a small nod of their head.

We dismounted at the town's plaza, tied the reins of our horses to a rail at its edge and walked into its centre. It was only a small square with the church and the Dominican

[5] *"Good afternoon"*

convent with its surrounding wall on one side and single storied shops and houses on the other three. It was not like the grand Plaza de Armes[6] I have seen in other towns and cities. There was no statue to a Conquistador, Liberator nor Inca; no fountain and as yet no grand official buildings. The pathways through the plaza seem to be in a grid pattern with a variety of tall trees and palms in between.

Don Alejandro was very proud of this little town. "We have a new Alcalde[7]. Well…he is still a priest and a gringo from Belgium, but he has assumed the position of Alcalde and has great

[6] *Literally "Arms Square" or "Parade Ground" which represented the first site of the military stockade established by the early Spanish settlers. Many Latin American cities or towns have a square thus named. Usually it will have the main church or cathedral on one side and the government offices on the opposite side. Shops usually occupy the other two sides.*
[7] *Mayor – In 1887 the Belgian priest Tomás Halflants assumed the position of Alcalde and built many buildings, bridges and began the construction of the Basilica of Nuestra Señora de Agua Santa*
[8]. *'Tresses of the Virgin'*

plans for the future of our town with the building of public works and a stone basilica in honour of our Virgin. And now our little city is a place of pilgrimage, Ecuadorians come to Baños de Agua and bathe in the waters at the base of the Cabellera de la Virgin[8], a small but beautiful waterfall. They light candles in the Santuario de la Virgen de Agua Santa and pray in the Basilica de la Virgen del Rosario de Agua Santa. Additionally, every October a festival is held in honour of the Virgin Mary."

We lunched at a small café with coffee and locro de papa[9] and bread. We paid our respects to the Virgin at the Basilica, then remounted before heading back east along the road to the hacienda. It had been a refreshing day for me, both in the good company of Don Alejandro, in

[9] *This is a famous Ecuadorian soup with avocados, potatoes and cheese.*

the fresh mountain air and the sights of the
lovely town and of the faith of the people of
Baños de Agua Santa.

Story Six

The Grandfather
(O Avô)

This story is set in the dark jungles of the Amazon in Brazil where Portuguese and native languages are spoken. It tells of one man's encounter with the harshness of the Amazon Basin and the spirit of the jungle.

They were seated on the little wooden veranda of the thatched hut which was perched rather precariously over a small lagoon on the edge of the jungle. The water of the lagoon was a still brown and was mostly covered with the very large, round water lily pads called Iaupê-Jaçanã[1] with their beautiful white flowers. Beyond the lagoon and through a wall of low, dense scrub

[1] *A Tupi-Guarani indigenous term meaning 'the lily trotter's waterlily' for the largest of all water lilies called in English 'which are called Victoria amazonica in honour of Queen Victoria.*

was the wide expanse of the Rio Negro which flows southeast into the mighty Amazon in this part of Brazil. There were heavy, black clouds coming up the river with lightning snaking brilliantly down to the dull grey water. Its thunder seemed to be reverberating off the tall trees of the jungle behind us, and the air was very still seeming to weigh heavily on our souls. The young soldier seated on the crude wooden bench next to the old man, took a small sip of the masato[2] beer which the old man had poured from a large earthenware jug, and looked down at the rough timber floor beneath his feet. "It was lucky that you were able to find us in that green hell of a jungle. Had not the Headquarters in Manaus asked for your help as a guide, my small patrol would be still wandering up and down the river."

[2] *Masato in is a fermented beverage common to many indigenous tribes in the Amazon and traditionally made with boiled cassava which is mixed with water, chewed in the mouth, spat out, and left to rest so that the cassava starch converts into sugar and alcohol.*

The old man refilled his wooden beaker with more of the masato from the jug and wiped his bearded mouth with the sleeve of his dirty shirt. "It was not luck, boy!" he said in his usual gruff voice for he had not liked being called out on to search for the small party of soldiers that had been sent out into the jungle south of the city several days ago. The young Lieutenant, whose men now shared his small hut and huddled together inside from the rain, looked up and smiled. "Yes. Thank you. If it was not for your skill in the jungle, we would have been lost."

The old man took a long swig of his drink then put the beaker down on the small table between them and looked intently at the young officer. "Yes, boy. It does take a lot of skill but something else other than mere luck to move through the forest. You are new to this country I think?" he said raising one bushy eyebrow. "And it is going to be a long night before this storm passes and you and your men can go back to Manaus. I will take you there myself in the morning as even this part of the tamed jungle can be treacherous to young fellows like you" he laughed. "Luck! Ha! You will need more than that if you wish to be a soldier in the forest. Your skills that they taught you in the Military Academy are not going to be much use unless you understand the Spirit of the Jungle."

The young soldier looked up at the old man's face which was like lined and hardened brown leather and which now bore a grave and serious expression. As his dark brown eyes looked out at the jungle beyond, they seemed to have almost a reflection of fear in them.

"The Spirit of the Jungle?" the young man enquired.

"Yes, my young senhor! The Spirit of the Jungle. Would you like to hear my story of how I met the Spirit of the Jungle?" the old man said leaning closely to his young guest. "It is a story of the past. My past! When I was a soldier like you! So, listen then and learn from an old man who has probably drunk too much masato, and lived in the jungle for too long."

To emphasise his story, the old man poured a liberal amount of masato into the young officer's beaker.

"I too, was just a young soldier those many years ago. I had just been made Cabo[3] and was on a patrol with our young Teniente into that green hell they call Amazonia. There was a problem with the Munduruku people who had been at peace with the colonialist for many years, but now were having their tribal lands invaded by those wishing to harvest the new wealth of rubber latex.

Our base was in the town of Itaituba on the Tapajós River, which is well to our south east, and a place where gold had been found. My

[3] *Corporal*

family had been in the district for many years, trading with the local Munduruku people and I had grown up playing with the local children. When I was of age, I joined the army and was able to stay in my town, eventually gaining some little promotion for I worked hard and had local knowledge. My grandfather had also been a scout and guide for the army many years at a time when the Munduruku were hostile to the new invaders, and the Jesuits who brought the word of a new god into the jungle." He took another mouthful of masato and looked down at his feet. "Our young Teniente was like you; very new at being a soldier and fresh out of the Academy at Rio de Janeiro. But he had come from a famous family of soldiers who had lived in this district for many years. Still, I did not feel that he had much confidence in himself, especially not where we were going. We had come from our barracks in Itaituba and followed the Rio Tapajós for a day, then started to cut our way through the jungle. It was very difficult, as the vegetation was thick, and many trees and bushes contained spikes to deter animals. Many of my companions had also not been in the jungle before as they had been recently posted from Santarém, the bigger city downstream which was very civilized, you understand?" The old man spat into the lagoon as if to express his dislike of big cities then continued:

"First, we lost one of our other Cabos, Diego Torres to a deadly fer-de-lance[4], and then our Sargento Balleña was taken by a caimán[5], when we were crossing a river. All of the time the insects - the mosquitos and gnats – and other nameless horrors were biting us, and keeping us awake at night. By the time we had finally reached our objective, which was a small hill a few kilometres south of what is now Aldeia,[6] Santa Maria, we were in a bad way. Our young

[4] *Literally "spearhead" and is a large, aggressive and venomous snake.*
[5] *A South American alligator.*
[6] *Portuguese for 'village'*

Teniente was now very afraid; he was lost now without the guidance of our Sargento Balleña. To make things worse, our native scouts had left us saying that the Munduruku were all around and after our blood."

The old man stood up and looked down the river into the heavy rain clouds which were rapidly approaching. He turned towards young officer and continued his story.

"It was raining there too, my boy, like it always does in the jungle when darkness falls. I was with the Teniente under a shelter which I had made from my cape and was trying to get a small fire going to make him some coffee. Suddenly he looked up over my shoulder, and loudly exclaimed 'Avô'!"[7]

His eyes were very wide, and I turned and saw a most fearsome sight. There, just in the faint

[7] *Grandfather.*

light of my small fire, at the edge of the bushes was an old man. He was a Blanco[8], like you my boy, but he was only wearing shorts and sandals, and his body was painted in black stripes from the juice of the huito plant,[9] like the natives do. His lower face was painted blue up past the eyes and his forehead was painted yellow. On this was painted a black snake. Now, I have never been afraid of much, having been raised in the jungle, but that night my hair stood on end, and I shivered in fear.

'Do not be afraid, meu Neto[10].' The old man said, 'for I have come to take you and your men home. There is an old trail nearby which the Munduruku women have made when they go foraging for their food. It is an old trail, but I

[8] *'White Man'*
[9] *["hwito"] or **Genipa americana** is a species of plant native to northern South America. It has many uses but the juice will stain the skin black.*
[10] *My Grandson.*

know it and the warriors nearby will not follow us for they are afraid of me.'

"Now young man! I now knew who this man really was! I had heard the stories from the old men in Itaituba about the wars with the Munduruku many years ago. There had been a famous leader of our patrols, who was the grandfather of our very own officer. This man, you understand, had grown up on the Rio Tapajós. It was a very wild place then, but this man had lived with his family on their plantation and had grown up with the boys of the local people. He learned everything there was about the jungle and its wild inhabitants. In time, this man became friends with an old Bruxo[11] who adopted him as his son and initiated him into his Anaconda Clan – that was the snake sign on his forehead.

---

[11] *["Brux-HO"] A shaman or traditional medicine man. Often belonging to secret clans.*

When hostilities broke out with a renegade group of the Munduruku, further to the north, this man joined the army and became a scout. The natives soon learned to be afraid of this man. He was a Bruxo, who could move quickly and unseen through the jungle. They called him Chullachaqui[12] – the Jungle Spirit, and he was death to them".

The young officer listened to this story with much interest and looked at the old man gazing down the river at the storm clouds. When the old man turned, he had a very serious and intense expression on his face. "Now boy, you really must understand what this term means, for it will show you the power of the man I talk about. Chullachaqui is not just a spirit living in the jungle, for there are many of these; it is the very spirit and life of the jungle itself. It can be a

12 *["Koola-KHAR–tee"] A Peruvian – Amazonian term is a malignant jungle spirit. Some myths describe it as an old man, others say that it is the embodiment of the jungle itself which pervades every living thing.*

very good spirit for those who know and practice its ways, but for an estranho[13] like ourselves, it can be a very bad spirit which is with you all the time you are in its land. Did you not feel him when you were lost in the jungle those many days"?

"Yes", the Lieutenant replied. "I do believe I know what you mean. Especially at night when the darkness closes in, and it is only the light from the fire which keeps fear at bay. It gives one a strong feeling of depression and foreboding. I never felt very happy at night in the jungle".

The old man nodded his head in agreement with this feeling and continued his story. "The Bruxo now told his grandson to get ready – 'we will go soon whilst the rain was still falling. Every man was to go, and litters were to be

---

[13] *Pronounced '[Is-tran-hyo'] for a stranger.*

made for those who could not walk. This man will come behind me and make a trail for you to follow,' the old Bruxo said, pointing to me. I was afraid, but stood and nodded that I would do as he asked.

So, with a new vigour and a fire in his eyes which I had never seen before, my young Teniente gathered the remains of our patrol, and I followed the old man into the darkness of the jungle. It seemed like many hours before the sun sent its feeble grey light through the trees, but we were going away from this hell, so time did not matter. The Munduruku did not come near as they were afraid of Chullachaqui, so we made good progress. We walked like this for several days, the old man leading at a fast pace, and in the closeness of the jungle I had great difficulty in keeping him in sight.

Once, when we had reached the open forest in view of our beloved Itaituba, he turned and looked at me. His stare was intense, but a smile came on his painted face. 'You are a good man. You have looked after my Neto so I will watch over you also.'

I thought at the time that this was a strange thing to say, but I put the thought aside and continued to follow him along the unseen trail. Eventually we came out of the forest and along a well-defined trail and into the outskirts of our town. The men were happy now, because they had been all afraid of the jungle and its stifling atmosphere, and now, they could breathe clean air again.

At the edge of the town, the old Bruxo had stopped. He gave his grandson one last long embrace, and with a wave of his hand, walked off back into the jungle.

So, we arrived back at our Company stockade and were greeted by our friends who had given us up for dead. After we had made our reports, and restored our bodies and souls, I made some coffee and took it to the young Teniente. I found him alone in his small room, sitting on his bed. He held a letter in his hand and tears were flowing freely."

Now my boy, I had seen this young officer change in the past few days from a frightened young man into a leader of men. Why did he have cause to cry?

'What is wrong, Teniente?' I asked. He handed me his letter, but I said 'Teniente, I am sorry, but I cannot read'.

He took the letter from my hand and looked up into my face with tears still in his eye. 'It is from my mother, Cabo.' he said. 'In it she tells me that her father, my grandfather, the man they called Chullachaqui, quietly passed away at his home in Santarém[14]. Before he died, she asked

14 *Santarém — a city almost 400 km downstream from Itaituba*

him to watch over me, her only son. She said that he smiled, closed his eyes and departed this world in peace'.

With an uncertain look he continued. 'Cabo, this letter arrived here only one day after we had started our patrol into the jungle.'

The old man sat down and took another swig from his beaker and then looked at the young lieutenant intently as though he wished to show him the importance of his story. "So, you see, my boy. It was not good fortune that led me to find you and your men in the jungle, but the old Bruxo – who had become for a while at least, the Spirit of the Jungle."

Story Seven:

The Gentleman of the Seas
(El Caballero de los Mares)

This is a true story of Peru's greatest naval hero who fought off the Chilean Navy during the War of the Pacific 1879 to 1884.

Our voyage so far had a pleasant one as the seas, for a change, along this rugged coastline of Peru, were calm for the most part. In one of the rare moments of meeting Captain Ridgeway on our short promenade deck, he informed us that, with the wind behind us and the Humboldt Current[1] running freely, we would be in Guayaquil, Ecuador by Tuesday morning.

---

[1] *The Humboldt or Peru Current is a cold, low-salinity ocean current that flows north along the western coast of South America and is named after the Prussian naturalist Alexander von Humboldt (1769 – 1859). The deserts of Peru and Chile are due to the current and prevailing winds which flow north and offshore rather than blow water eastward onto the land.*

That evening at dinner, the captain, as was his nightly custom, called upon his youngest officer, Mister Connor, the American, to give a toast to the British king, Edward the Seventh whose portrait took pride of place on the bulkhead behind the head of the table. It was strange for us, being raised in the polite societies of our countries to make such a toast without standing. But the good captain had explained that it was an old custom in which he had been indoctrinated whilst in the Royal Navy, to make such toasts in the sitting position since the days when King William the Fourth had witnessed a young officer cracking his head on the deckhead[2] upon standing to give such a toast whilst serving with the Royal Navy over one hundred years ago.

It being Sunday, Mister Connor also gave the Toast for the Day which was 'to absent friends'.

---

[2] *Deckhead is the ceiling of any ship's cabin as opposed to bulkhead which are the walls. In early sailing ships, the deckhead was often much less than the height of a standing person.*

It seemed strange to us also that an American should be giving the toasts appropriate to the British Royal Navy, but Captain Ridgeway gave a simple justification for his custom by saying that this was a British ship and that he himself had been in the Royal Navy or 'the Andrew[3]' as he called it, in his youth.

Dinner on Sunday nights also seemed to be one of the captain's traditions which consisted of a lamb roast with all the usual English trimmings of baked vegetables, green beans, Yorkshire pudding, gravy and mint sauce. At least there was an excellent Argentinian Malbec[4] to complement the food.

After dinner, Captain Ridgeway stood up, the deckhead being just a short distance above his head and announced that it was also the custom

[3] *The most common theory is that the Royal Navy is named after Lieutenant Andrew Miller, a fervent and fearsome officer in the Impress Service which forcibly 'recruited' men as sailors.*
[4] *Malbec is a red wine. The grapes are known as one of the six grapes used in the blend of red Bordeaux wine. It is also celebrated as an Argentine variety of grape.*

for an after-dinner speech to be given by one of the officers. Tonight, it was the turn of the Second Officer Mister Rodríguez. Applause as the captain sat down.

Mister Rodríguez, to use his formal maritime rank rather than his Spanish honorific of 'Señor', stood up and pulled a small sheet of paper from his tunic. He was a tall, thin man with the complexion of a southern European, that is with pale brown skin, brown eyes and black hair which glistened with a light application of hair tonic. He had thin, black pencil moustaches and I could not help thinking that he would be more at home in the salons of Lima than from the small coastal village of Arica, now part of Chile, where he had been born. He seemed quite young for the rank of Second Officer; I guessed that he would be no more than in his late twenties.

He cleared his throat and looked around the table with his dark, penetrating eyes.

"Señora y Señores..." he said, lapsing into his native tongue "...forgive me. Ladies and gentlemen, it is my honour to give the Sunday speech," he continued in good English.

"As we are still in Peruvian waters, I would like to talk about one of our great heroes of the most recent War of the Pacific. I do this as a Peruvian and in deference to our guests here tonight who are also from my country. May I ask if any of you gentlemen do not speak the English?" he looked rather earnest with this question and he seemed now more like an undergraduate student giving his fist dissertation rather than a lothario from Lima.

One of the gentlemen sitting near Captain Ridgeway and obviously a man of importance gave a brief nod of his head and said in good English." Thank you, Señor Rodríguez, I believe that many of our countrymen here speak English, but I would be delighted to give a brief and progressive translation if one is necessary. Please continue."

"Muchas gracias, Doctor Vázquez." He replied with a small bow to the gentleman concerned whom he knew to be a surgeon from Lima. "I will now tell you the story of Almirante Miguel Grau Seminario, Peru's most famous sailor; the man that both the Peruvian and Chilean Navies called 'el Caballero de los Mares', or in English, 'the Gentleman of the Seas'."

The young officer lowered his eyes which were now wet with tears. "I had the honour to be a very young 'Alférez de Fragata', or as you would say 'Second Lieutenant' at the time." He looked over at the captain, "I do not think that we had a rank equal to your Midshipman but anyway, I had the lowest rank of officer in the navy, and it was my first posting, you understand."

The young officer then consulted his notes, but I think that his story came more from his heart than from his sheet of paper. He went on and gave his story about the Gentleman of the Seas.

"Almirante Miguel Grau was born in the coastal town of Paita, which we will be passing tomorrow, in 1834. He entered the Paita Nautical School and first went to sea when he was nine years old, aboard a merchant schooner and later in other sailing vessels as he sailed all over the world. In 1853, at the age of 19, he left the merchant marine and became an officer in the Peruvian Navy. His career was brilliant, and promotion was rapid."

The young man consulted his notes as he continued. "In 1868, he was named commander of the *Huáscar*[5] with the rank of Lieutenant Commander and was later promoted to Commander. By 1874, he had become the commanding officer of all the Peruvian Navy's fleet with the rank of Captain.

The *Huáscar* was our navy's flagship and was an ironclad turret vessel, that is, it was built of iron and had its main armament in a revolving turret

[5] *Huáscar (1503–1532) was the Inca who succeeded his father, Huayna Capac and ruled the Incan Empire from 1527 to 1532.*

on the deck. It was also equipped with a most formable ram in its bow. Some in other navies would call it a turret-ram. It was built in Britain by John Laird Sons & Company and launched at Birkenhead in Cheshire in 1865. It was named after one of our rulers of the sixteenth century, the Inca Huáscar. I have some details of her construction if you are interested?"

Without waiting for a reply, he pulled another card from his tunic pocket and continued his talk. "She was described as being of 1,100 tons' displacement, with steam engines of 1500-horsepower driving a screw propeller which gave a speed of about 12 knots. She was 190 feet[6] in length, 35 feet in breadth, and 19 feet 9 inches in depth. She carried two Armstrong breech-loading 10-inch guns in one turret, several smaller canons on deck and a Gatling gun."

---

[6] *There are approximately 3.3 feet in one metre with 12 inches to the foot.*

There was a general hubbub around the table as some of the other guests made comments about the effectiveness of such a fighting ship. Second Officer Rodríguez continued his story:

"When the War of the Pacific began on 5th April 1879, between Chile and Peru which had come to the aid of Bolivia whose coastal territory had been invaded, Miguel Grau was aboard the *Huáscar*, as its captain. In an impressive display of naval mastery, Capitán Grau then played an important role interrupting Chilean lines of communication and supply, damaging, capturing or destroying several enemy vessels, and bombarding port installations. The *Huáscar* soon became famed for striking by surprise; these actions initially prevented a Chilean invasion by sea. For his actions, Capitán Grau was promoted to the rank of Contralmirante - that is the equivalent to Rear Admiral in the British Navy. Very soon, on the 21st of May, the *Huáscar* came out of a thick sea fog and encountered the Chilean wooden steam corvette, the *Esmeralda*, captained by Arturo Prat Chacón, and two other vessels: the schooner the

Covadonga and the transport *La Mar* in the bay at Iquique. Now this town was once part of our Peru but was being blockaded by the Chilean ships. It is now part of Chile and about two hundred nautical miles[7] south of Matarani, now the major port of southern Peru."

Second Officer Rodríguez looked over at one of the young passengers, a lawyer, seated at the table with a look of enthusiasm and said, "You, Señor Porteños might be interested to know that the Chilean, Capitán Arturo Prat was also a lawyer! He studied whilst he was a naval officer and was accepted as a lawyer in 1876. He wanted to be a naval lawyer and made several reforms to the Chilean Navy's legal codes but regrettably he died before he could complete his work."

Señor Porteños blushed slightly as he had followed a similar course in the army of Peru and had finally succeeded in reaching his goal as a military lawyer.

---

[7] *One nautical mile is about 1.8 kilometres.*

The Second Officer continued his story: "Now, the *Huáscar* came upon the Chilean ships quite unexpectedly and the two smaller vessels turned and fled further into the bay leaving the *Esmeralda* alone to fight the *Huáscar*. This poor ship was doomed from the start: she was wooden against the *Huáscar's* armoured iron plate; she was smaller in size and with smaller calibre cannon. She could also only travel at eight knots as opposed to the *Huáscar's* twelve.

Now the *Huáscar* had been accompanied by the Peruvian ironclad the *Independencia* captained by Juan Guillermo More who was ordered by Almirante Grau to pursue and sink the other fleeing Chilean ships. At a critical moment however, the helmsman of *Independencia* was shot by a sharpshooter aboard the Chilean ship *Covadonga* and, out of control, the *Independencia* ran aground.

Meanwhile, Capitán Prat had manoeuvred the *Esmeralda* so that it was near the coast, but Grau moved in and began firing with his big guns at six hundred metres. The Chileans returned fire, but their smaller shells simply bounced off the *Huáscar's* armour plate. To add to Capitán Prat's worries, the Peruvians on the shore had set up field artillery on the beach and a fortuitous shot had hit the *Esmeralda,* causing one of her boilers to explode. More shells from the *Huáscar* hit the unfortunate wooden vessel killing several of its crew. Now only able to steam at two knots, Prat manoeuvred his ship so than it was between the *Huáscar* and the Peruvian shore batteries. Unable to effectively use his cannons and wanting to prevent anymore slaughter, Grau ordered his ship to ram the *Esmeralda* which it did at full speed.

It was said that on the impact between the two ships, the brave Capitán Prat jumped aboard the *Huáscar* with the cry of 'follow me, boys!' he was followed by Petty Officer Juan de Dios Aldea. But the two men found that they were alone as the noise of battle prevented the rest of the crew of the *Esmeralda* hearing Capitán Prat's words. Prat was immediately shot to death on the deck near the turret by one of the sharpshooters on the *Huáscar* and the gallant Petty Officer was severely wounded.

Grau gave orders for the *Huáscar* to stand off and allow the remainder of the crew of the *Esmeralda* to surrender. They did not and fought on under the command of the ship's only surviving officer, Lieutenant Luis Uribe Orrego who had the Chilean flag nailed to the mizzen[8] mast.

The *Esmeralda* was rammed again but this time Sub-lieutenant Ignacio Serrano of that ship boarded *Huáscar* with eleven more men, armed with machetes and rifles but the Gatling gun of the *Huáscar* cut them down leaving only Sub-lieutenant Serrano the only survivor, with several shot wounds in the groin. Grau gave orders that he should be carried below to the infirmary and treated alongside Petty Officer Aldea. Not long afterwards, after being battered for over four hours the gallant *Esmeralda* sank below the waters of Iquique Bay, the Chilean

[8] *The rear mast of a ship*

flag still nailed to the mizzen mast flying until the waves broke over it.

Almirante Grau, distressed at the plight of the very few survivors of the *Esmeralda* now fighting for their lives amidst the turmoil where their ship had gone down; ordered the boats of the *Huáscar* to be lowered to take the survivors aboard to be given all medical aid and comfort. They were our enemies but now just drowning men who must be saved from the sea. Out of a compliment of over two hundred men, only fifty-seven were rescued. Having secured all the men and bodies which we could, our ship headed for our companion, the luckless *Independencia* which was aground. We took off her crew and then set her alight so that she would not fall into enemy hands.

After the battle and the lifting of the blockade of the town of Iquique, Almirante Grau sent Prat's personal effects such as his diary, uniform and sword among other items, to his widow in Chile. He also attached a personal letter describing the heroism of her husband and his own personal sadness in seeing the death of such a gallant officer, offering any assistance which was able to give. Grau also had the bodies of the dead Chilean sailors buried with full military honours on the shore of the bay. Because of his actions in the battle and later for his noble gestures toward Prat's widow and the surviving crew members, Grau became honoured in both Peru and Chile as a gallant naval hero and was now known by all as the "Gentleman of the Seas"."

There was applause around the table as the Second Officer sat down. Captain Ridgeway stood up: "Thank you, Mister Rodríguez for your most stirring personal account of the Battle of Iquique." He looked around the table and asked if any of us had any comments.

Mister Henry Radcliffe, a merchant from Leeds, England beamed across the table and said: "What a grand event that battle must have been! Your story, Mister Rodríguez reminded me of the tales my father used to tell me when I was a boy. He sailed with Nelson; don't you know? Thank you for your account, sir."

The Second Officer looked over at our party sitting opposite with some anticipation of receiving some comment from his fellow countrymen, so the surgeon, Doctor Vázquez stood up.

"Señor Rodríguez, on behalf of my companions, may I congratulate you on your most exciting and gratifying story of one of Peru's greatest sailors, Almirante Grau Seminario, el Caballero de los Mares. Of course, even in the high Altiplano we have heard of his gallant exploits but not as well told as we heard tonight. Thank you. But tell me, since you were aboard her, what was the true fate of the *Huáscar*? The popular press only ever provides details of the victories in warfare, very rarely the defeats. We know, of course that she was eventually captured but for our curiosity and for the edification of Señor Radcliffe, perhaps you could enlighten us on that event?"

The Second Officer looked at his captain who smiled and gave a brief nod of his head. Rodríguez again stood up but looked sad, again his dark brown eyes had a watery gaze. "Muchas gracias, Doctor Vázquez. It was a very heroic tale and a sad one. Regrettably I cannot give you a first-hand account of the end of the *Huáscar* as I was on shore during the final days of my ship. I was the Signal Officer during the Battle of Iquique and spent most of my time in the armoured casement of the bridge with the Almirante. Unfortunately, when taking a message to the gunnery officer in the turret, our communications tube having been shot away, I received a slight wound and was taken to the infirmary. After the battle, the Almirante insisted that I be taken ashore with the rest of the wounded and given all the best care. He even wrote to my mother. The ship then sailed without me! Luckily, I was evacuated from the hospital at Iquique and taken north before the Chileans overran the town in November."

The Second Officer hung his head and waited for a short time until his sadness passed, then he continued. "I will keep this story very brief, if you do not mind. After I was taken ashore, my ship, the *Huáscar*, sailed south to continue to harass the Chilean supply ships; she even captured a transport full of a regiment of cavalry. However, the Chileans eventually could not tolerate her interference any longer and sent a small fleet out to rid themselves of this lone raider. A few months later, in October of 1879, off Punta Angamos, which is about forty nautical miles north of Antofagasta, the *Huáscar* accompanied by the corvette *Unión*, encountered the entire Chilean fleet. This was under the command of Commodore Galvarino Riveros who had with him six ships including two armoured steam frigates, the flagship *Blanco Encalada* and the *Almirante Cochrane* captained by Commander Juan Jose Latorre. These two ships engaged the *Huáscar* whilst our speedier *Unión* was able to fight her way through the cordon and sail north to Arica.

Right from the outset, the heavier guns of the Chilean frigates caused considerable damage to the poor *Huáscar*. A shot from the *Cochrane* pierced *Huáscar*'s turret, wounding the twelve crew members manning the 300-pound cannons. Another shot perforated the armour just above the waterline, cutting the rudder chain leaving *Huáscar* temporarily adrift. Soon after, an armour-piercing shell from *Cochrane* struck the bridge casement, killing Almirante Grau, but the *Huáscar* fought on.

With the Almirante, her Captain and many of her crew killed or wounded, Lieutenant Pedro Garezon, now in command decided to scuttle the ship. Seeing the bad state of the ship, the Chileans closed in and boarded the *Huáscar* taking her gallant crew prisoners. The remains of Almirante Grau were taken ashore and buried in Chile with full military honours. In recognition of her gallantry, the *Huáscar* was taken into the Chilean Navy where she still serves as a reminder of her gallant defeat[9]." The Second Officer sat down and for a while there was silence.

[9] *Today (2025) the Huáscar is preserved as a museum ship and shrine in the Chilean port of Talcahuano*

Captain Ridgeway stood up, coughed and said. "Madam Radcliffe, gentlemen, perhaps we should all adjourn to the rear of the saloon where I notice that Filipe has set out our coffee."

We stood up and made our way from the dining table. It was only then that I noticed that our tall Second Officer walked proudly, but with a distinct limp.

Story Eight:

The Simpleton of Yanahuara
(El Simplón de Yanahuara)

Not all heroes are found on the deck of a fighting ship nor leading their troops against a determined enemy on land. Some heroes are just ordinary people who find that they must act in extraordinary situations.

It was going to be a good day; the air was clear, and the sunlight was shining brightly on the grey cobbles of the street which bordered the Plaza de Armes[1] in Puno, the main city siting on the edge of Lake Titicaca in the high Andes of Peru. The two men sat enjoying the cool of the morning, watching the local people carrying their sacks of produce to the market on the edge of the square.

[1] *'Arms Square' where the Spaniards originally set up their fort but is now the name used for the main square in many South American cities.*

The elder of the two men, whose name was Rodrigo, offered the other a cigar and lit it for him with from an old tinder box. As they sat enjoying the fragrance of the tobacco their peace was interrupted by the passing of a small cart. It was a simple vehicle with plain, homemade wheels and plain wooden sides. It was the cart which had come from a nearby village, bringing fresh fruit and vegetables for the market in the plaza. On the seat of the cart were two men. One was an old man with grey whiskers, wearing a faded black hat made of old felt and a tattered brown poncho. Next to him slouched a young man, hatless, his hair a lank brown which hung loosely down his face. The cart stopped opposite the two men enjoying their cigars allowing the young man on the cart to slowly climb down.

"Ah, look Don Rodrigo, the youngster is a simpleton." His companion pointed out.

Rodrigo watched the young man in question help the older man down from the cart and arm in arm they shuffled together to its rear to fetch the baskets of produce.

"Yes, I think that you are right." He replied.

"What a shame, Señor. To have such a burden to live with." Rodrigo's young companion lamented with some compassion.

"That may be true for some people" the old man replied, "especially for those who feel that it is because of their own sins. They feel that they must wear their child's affliction like a hair coat and suffer with it. Many people, however, learn to live with the situation and eventually see that such people – whom we call simpletons and other names – also have a place in this world. It is said that they are the Children of God and through them we can see God's heart."

"Perhaps you are right, Don Rodrigo." The younger man said now looking at the ground and feeling a little self-conscious.

"Perhaps" Rodrigo replied. "But then I am but an old man and all old men are like storekeepers – they weigh everything and think too much about what the world should be like rather than what it is. I believe that having spent all of our younger years trying to be acceptable to others we lose all of those good virtues which we had as children, especially love for all of those around us and faith in what we are told. We also lose some of our care and helpfulness to all others who are in need and of course, our we lose our innocence. By that I mean our innocence in thought by looking at everything simply and sometimes finding uncomplicated solutions to our problems. I believe that people like the young man yonder still see the world like a small child. They give love and tenderness without reservation or shame." Old Rodrigo took out his cigar and nodded to the two men at their cart. Look at the way he helps the old man. "Perhaps the old man is his father or grandfather, but he shows his love for the older man by his careful assistance."

Rodrigo's young friend now looked at the pair, just a simpleton and an old man.

Old Rodrigo continued. "These two remind me of a story which I was told, a long time ago. It certainly changed my outlook towards such men. Would you like to hear it?"

"Oh yes!" His young friend said with enthusiasm. "I always like to listen to your stories. A young man like me, with very little education has a lot he can learn by such stories."

"Well then, my young friend!" Rodrigo continued." This is a story of the simpleton of Yanahuara[2]. It was told to me by the Sacristan of the Church of Saint John the Baptist at Arequipa, a long way from here down the mountains where I once lived. I do not think that you have been there, as it is on the western side of the Andes east of Puno about two days' travel. It is at about two and a half thousand metres above sea level.

It is a beautiful city within sight of three active volcanoes: the rugged shapes of Pichu Pichu, Chachani and the mighty cone of El Misti. The city is built on the slopes of El Misti and the river Chili comes down off its slopes and flows through the city. All of our country's western slopes of the Andes are deserts and it is only because of rivers like this that such cities can

[2] *This is the Spanish equivalent of the indigenous name Yanawara and refers to the tribe of people living in that barrio or neighbourhood.*

survive. The city is mostly made of fine stone with cobbled streets and a large Plaza de Armes with a large cathedral on one side and the government buildings on the other. Joining the two on each side of the plaza are colonnaded buildings which house a number of shops. The authorities in Arequipa are proud of their city and call it the 'White City' because of the beautiful buildings which are made from the fine white volcanic rock from the mountains. However, some say that this name was used in jest by the early indigenous people such as the Yanahuara, to mean that it is the city where the 'blancos', or white people, that is the Spaniards, lived.

The barrio where I stayed was called 'Yanahuara' after the tribe who lived in the region. Their name 'Yanahuara' possibly is Quechua for 'those who wear black short trousers'."

The young man grinned at that, for he spoke Quechua as his native tongue, although a northern dialect of it, and he replied. "Black shorts! That would be interesting to see."

"Well." Rodrigo continued. "It would be what they were used to. Our Andean peoples wear many different types of costume as you well know and we can often tell from which village they come, by their dress. It may be a head covering, shawl or trousers but that is what they are happy in. You know, on the isle of Taquile in Lake Titicaca where the men do the knitting, the women know which men are available for marriage by the colour and form of their soft caps - it identifies his relationship status. If a cap is coloured red and white it means he is single, red and blue means he is engaged and all red means he is married. Furthermore, the direction of the extended top is the way to express a man's current state of mind. If the top is laid to the right side, it means he is happy and content. Left side indicates he's worrying about something and wants to keep the problems away. The most common, especially when they are knitting, is the hat top to the back. This means they are busy.

Well then, to my story. I had gone to Arequipa for some reason or another to do with my civilian occupation as a merchant. Perhaps it was to sell some alpaca wool. I do not recall. I stayed in a small posada in the district of Yanahuara, which is to the northwest of the Plaza de Armes, and went to Mass at the Church of Saint John the Baptist which was nearby. This is a beautiful church built over one hundred years ago also of the fine, white stone of the mountains. It has a good square tower, and the portico is finely decorated. Here I met the old Sacristan, and we became good friends over the short time of my stay. Perhaps he was sympathetic to my enquiring nature or perhaps it was that he had a good story to tell a newcomer, I do not know, but he told me a story which showed the nature of one such Child of God. This is his story:"

"I am an old man now, but in my youth, I also attended this church. I was a choirboy and went to the little school behind the building run by the good Sisters. At this time there was a poor labourer who worked for the church and lived in a small hovel just down the hill. As you see, the church is built on a high ridge which runs down to the terraced fields built by the Old People.

Now this man had a son called Juan who was a simpleton. He went to our school but the Sisters found him a very difficult student. Oh, it was not because he was a bad child. Far from it! He was quiet and gentle in nature and always had a big smile. Sister Amelia was always upset at this. She would come into the classroom and Juan would be leaning on his desk with his mouth open in this idiotic smile and saliva drooling out of the corner of his mouth.

'Ugh, Juan! Close your mouth.' She would say, and we would all laugh. Juan would laugh too, as it was not in his nature to take offence. We would call him 'Loco Juan' or 'el Tonto[3]' behind his back. Some of the rowdier children would often play tricks on him, but he just smiled and would quietly go about his business. Children can be very cruel at times.

His mother had died when he was in his infancy – perhaps she could not bear the thought of having a simpleton – but his father loved him dearly and would do his best to give his only

[3] *'The fool'*

son a good life. The good Sisters tried too, but their attempts to teach him his letters simply went astray. Eventually he left our small school and helped his father in his small tasks of maintaining the church. Sometimes he would take his small cart around the streets carrying whatever he could for the older people and the lame as well as picking up any discarded item which might be of value. Sometimes he would go down the hill and help the farmers cultivate their corn and potatoes in the old, terraced gardens.

Juan was not a big lad like most of his former classmates. He was thin and not very tall. His skin eventually was burnt to the hard brown colour of the labourer and his sparse hair hung down, long and untidy. One thing that his father was able to teach his son was a love of music. In the evenings when their work for the day had been done, they would sit on the edge of the ridge and the old man would teach his son to play the tarqa[4], and also sing some of the old songs of the Yanahuara people. Some unkind souls would say that in both these two things the old man failed. Oh, Juan could play the tarqa, and also sing but neither was harmonious or with any gusto. But Juan and the old man were happy and lived quietly in their small house near the church.

When the old man died – Juan would have been aged about thirty – he was distraught and mourned his father for a long time. The priest saw to it that the old man had a good funeral, and the good Sisters did all they could for poor Loco Juan. One of the wealthier parishioners who had appreciated the old man's help paid for a small vault in the long panel of raised vaults which are the custom here as the ground is very hard.

I think that they are better than the ugly graves which are dug into the ground." The Sacristan

4 *The tarqa (Quechua, Aymara) is a flute of the Andes. Made of wood, it has 6 finger holes, a mouthpiece to blow across on one end and free hole on the other.*

continued. "In front of the small wall in front of the coffin and behind a nice sheet of glass we can put small mementos of the departed and perhaps a small likeness. Juan's father's window had a small cart, and some little flowers made from cloth which one of the good Sisters found in the church.

So Loco John continued his father's work – he had no other skills – but he was a different character to his father. He would pull his little cart around the streets playing his tarqa and singing his strange little songs but always he had a big grin and a cheerful 'Hola![5]' to all he passed. The dogs in the streets would come to him with their tails all wagging and it often seemed that the birds in the sky would sing with him. By now, the rest of us boys had also grown up and were too intent with learning the skills of manhood to pay much attention to Juan. Oh, there were a few who would still shout abuse at him to enlarge their own feelings of self-importance, but most people were kind

[5] *'Hello!'*

to Loco Juan. He became part of the local scenery. He would come down the same street at about the same time and help all those who needed him. He would carry some of the baskets of the womenfolk who went down the hill to barter for vegetables from the farmers on the terraces. He would help anyone who needed a hand. He never asked for any money but was always thankful when someone gave him a few coins or some food in exchange for his labours. On Saturdays, Juan would leave his little cart at home and wander through the streets singing his funny songs but in a soft voice so as not to disturb anyone. Sometimes people would come to their gate and wish him well and he did not mind the name of 'Loco Juan'. He would return their salutes with a cheerful 'buenas dias[6]' and continue on his way.

In the afternoon, he would take his little cart out of the barrio and up the road which lead to the local refuse mound. Here he would look for anything of value which he might sell to the

[6] *'Good day!'*

traders along the street of the Puente[7] Bolagnesi which crosses the Rio Chili and then goes up the hill to the Plaza de Armes in the centre of the city.

Of all of the items which Loco Juan scavenged from the refuse mound, his most prized items where the old bottles which had been discarded over the centuries. He rarely sold those but kept them on shelves along the wall of his shack. I know, because when I became the new Sacristan – I was much younger then – I went with Father Benedict one day to offer some pastoral care, we saw Juan's fine collection of old bottles. He would sometimes pass by an antique shop with one of his latest finds and ask the opinion of the owner. As everyone liked Loco Juan he would get an honest reply and sometimes an offer to buy, but he rarely sold.

Now Fate often leads man along unexpected paths. One day Juan went off his usual route and down a street which led to a wealthier part of the city in the barrio of Jose Luis Bustamante

7 Bridge

y Rivero. Here were some grand houses which were from the colonial times. They had large front gates and gardens which were overlooked by beautiful balconies. Juan wandered down this street singing his quiet song and a few people came out to see who it was. Some smiled and wished him a good day but others went back inside and loudly closed their shutters. At one large and imposing house a lady saw Juan passing and called for him to wait. Soon a maid came out and offered Juan a cool drink. This was something new to Juan and the lady was the most beautiful woman that he had ever seen. He was entranced. After that day he would regularly wander down that street, hoping that he would see the beautiful lady again.

This lady was Señora Valentina Medina Campos, the wife of Coronel Fernando Medina Montero, a most disagreeable man. He was despised by his troops for his aggressive character and poor leadership and by his peers for his arrogance. It was difficult to believe that such a beautiful woman, both in appearance and spirit would marry such a man. Perhaps he may have been a dashing officer in his youth or perhaps the marriage had been arranged. Who knows?

Whatever the reason, Doña Valentina was loved by all she met. She was always there if a friend or neighbour needed help, and she always had a smile on her beautiful face. No problem was too great a burden for her to solve with a laugh and a smile. Perhaps she felt sorry for poor Loco Juan and that is why she often would send her maid down to the gate to offer him a cool drink if it was warm or an extra coat if it was cold. Anyway, Juan became a regular visitor to that street and the others in the neighbourhood soon became at least tolerant of his poor tarqa playing and raucous songs.

No-one really knows what happened on that fateful day. Some say that Doña Valentina was at the gate farewelling her husband who was going to his regiment when Loco Juan came down the street. Don Fernando did not like a simpleton such as Juan and all of those who were not to his standard of perfection. He reined his horse around to push the simpleton away with Doña Valentina still clutching his saddle. The Colonel beat his wife with his riding crop and brave Juan tried to stop him but was caught unawares and fell beneath the hooves of the Colonel's horse. The Colonel continued to trample the horse over the poor man and in desperation, Doña Valentina pulled the pistol out of the Colonel's holster with both hands pleading with her husband to stop. Alas, the pistol accidently discharged, and the Colonel fell from his horse which then bolted down the street.

At the sound of the gunshot, many people ran into the street. Doña Valentina had crumpled to the ground to console her dying husband, but the simpleton lay still on the cobbles. Someone sent for a doctor and a priest but only the priest was needed. Father Benedict came quickly and gave the last rites to the Colonel and Juan whilst Doña Valentina's maid took her into the house. The Colonel's body was carried into the house by his servants and Juan's body was placed carefully onto his little cart by some of the men who had run into the street. With the help of some of these men, Father Benedict wheeled the little cart containing Loco Juan's body back to his little hovel down the hill from the church.

The Colonel was later buried by his regiment's Chaplain in a quiet ceremony with only Doña Valentina, her maid and a few officers who were there out of duty rather than compassion for their colleague. Juan had had a more elaborate ceremony at this church with many people from Yanahuara coming to pay their respects. Some money was raised, and Juan's body was interred in a vault above the ground not far that of his father. In the glass front of the vault, they put a small wooden model of a cart, his tarqa and several small painted flowers made of wood which the children of the orphanage had carved. It is never without flowers in the vases at the front of the vault."

"And what happened to the poor wife, Doña Valentina?" I had replied.

"Ah" said the Sacristan." That is the only good which came from this sad event. She sold all of her possessions and gave the money to the poor of the city. She took her maid and entered the Monasterio de Santa Catalina[8] not far from the cathedral and the Plaza de Armes. From here she was able to visit many of the sick and poor of the city in honour of poor Loco Juan and in penitence for the death of her husband. She became very well known for her good works and the people called her 'La Doña Blanca[9]'.

Old Rodrigo sat back and took a quick puff of his cigar, "So my young friend! That is my story of Loco Juan of Yanahuara. Poor John was a simpleton to be sure, but he was greatly loved for his infectious happy innocence, his helpfulness and his final act of bravery."

[8] *The Monastery of Saint Catherine was founded in 1580 by a rich widow, Doña María de Guzmán. The nuns are of the Dominican Second Order and those pious young ladies who were admitted were of the upper classes who were housed in good quarters and were allowed to take some servants with them. The Monastery today is more of a tourist attraction.*
[9] *'The White Lady'*

Rodrigo looked over and nodded towards the young simpleton helping the old man with his cartload of vegetables. "So, what do you see there?" he said.

The young man looked up and wiped a small tear from his eye "Now I see just a man helping another. I do not see a simpleton anymore." He replied.

"Yes! That is what we all should see" Rodrigo continued. "We are all of God's children but some, like that young man and poor Loco Juan continue to be full of His grace, even when the rest of us, having grown to manhood, have lost many of the virtues which He gave us. In many ways it is sad that we are not more like the simpleton of Yanahuara."

Story Nine

The Golden Chalice
(El Cáliz Dorado)

This is a simple story of faith set in a seminary high in the Andes Mountains in Chile. In these mountains where life is often hard, but proceeds are a slower pace, the old ways are often still practiced and the old languages still spoken.

It was in Matteo's second year at the small seminary of San Isidro in the central mountains of Chile in the Year of Our Lord 1884. It was at that time when an event occurred which shocked most of the good people of the nearby town of Los Olmos.

As part of its social commitment to the local community, the seminary had a day in which relatives and guests could come and visit its main buildings and mix socially for a short time with its students. It was always a good time for the local people and sometimes people from afar would also come to visit their relatives and to see how the seminary operated.

This was a happy day for most of the students, except for Matteo whose family lived far away in the city of Santiago and were usually too busy to travel. His only contact was from the few letters written by his sister, Gabriella and on some rare occasions from his younger brother, Alejandro.

However, he had a very enquiring mind and was always interested in his studies of natural science and investigation. He had also made several close friends at the seminary in Felipe Ortega and Antonio Jiménez.

Ortega was the son of a merchant from Valparaíso but had always wanted to be a priest. His family was wealthy one who traced their ancestry back to some of the early Spanish settlers in Chile. Tall and slender, there was something of the ascetic about him and Matteo liked his thoughtfulness and learning.

Jiménez was a total contrast to his friend and came from a small farm not far from the hamlet of Parinacota far to the north in the mountains near the border with Bolivia. He was of the Aymara people and hoped to return to the district to serve there as a priest. Being of a quick intelligence, he had received some patronage from his Parish and from some wealthy merchants in the town who wished to promote the welfare of the local people. He was a cheerful fellow, typical of many Andinos[1] who always had a good story to tell and at home would always have a jar of freshly brewed chicha[2] on hand.

There was another seminarian with whom Matteo sometimes shared some time; mainly in study or deep and often aggravated discussion about some theological point of view. Antonio Navarro Torres, to give him his full Spanish

[1] *A general term here for any people who live in the high Andes Mountains.*
[2] *A corn beer brewed at home and commonly found in many communities in the Andes.*

name, was friendly enough with Matteo but did not socialise with most of the other seminarians, especially Matteo's other two close friends. He kept mostly to himself but often sought Matteo's opinion on intellectual matters. Matteo felt sorry for this young man, feeling that he was a troubled soul and would probably not survive the rigors of his studies. For his part, Navarro expressed confidence in his future but spent much of his contact with Matteo talking about his wealthy and noble family in Santiago who were descended from one of the first Conquistadores to come to Chile with Diego de Almagro in 1540. Matteo, at times felt the need to council him when he expressed a low opinion of the local people; hardly that of a future priest!

Now in the chapel, there were several chalices sitting on a silver tray on the altar. Most of them were of simple earthenware which had been made by several of the Andino peoples who lived within the region and bore many of the traditional symbols of those people. One. However, was of gold. This had been donated by a wealthy family, the Clemente family, and was reputed to have been of Incan origin, looted from some palace centuries ago. The chalices were used for various feast days as part of the Sacrament, the golden chalice being reserved for Christmas and Easter services.

Not long after the seminary had opened its doors to visitors, the golden chalice was found to be missing. The discovery was made when the chapel was being cleaned and readied for the evening devotions. Immediately the Rector was notified, and a thorough search was made by the priests and brothers of the teaching staff. When the chalice was not found in the chapel nor the sacristy, there had been no alternative but to search the rest of the seminary, including the cells of its students. Nothing was found and so the local Prefecture was called in to make a more thorough search and to make enquires about the city. The news soon spread rapidly through the area, and everyone was dismayed that such a theft could occur within a seminary.

Matteo was, like the other seminarians, dismayed too, but decided to look into the matter himself. There were no obvious suspects, so he had to make some general observations and his own private search of the common areas of each building.

On the evening of the second day, Matteo was sitting in a quiet corner of the seminary library when Antonio Navarro sat down next to him. The young man seemed agitated and asked Matteo if he had heard of any news from the Prefecture about the missing chalice.

"No, not yet," said Matteo in a casual tone.

"There were too many visitors here the other day. Especially some of the local people. They are simple people, poor to boot. A golden chalice like that would set them and their families up for life."

Matteo was rather shocked and dismayed at this comment, not only because of his own ancestry, which was both Spanish and Mapuche, but because he knew that such common and brazen thieving was not in the usual character of the people of the Andes. He looked across at Navarro and told him so.

The young man did not like to be reproached and so he stood up, glared at Matteo for a short moment and then stormed out of the library. Matteo felt that such a comment and the young man's attitude was worth further investigation.

Matteo did not suspect any of the recent visitors to the seminary, as few had visited the chapel alone; mostly coming in and staying with their relatives or other seminarians. On that day, there had always been a seminarian in the chapel to explain to the visitors the various paintings and artefacts which were contained within it, including the tray of chalices. He himself had been given such a task during the morning and his friends had also shared in this responsibility. The chalice must have been taken late in the afternoon when most of the guests had departed.

Matteo made another general search of the chapel, library, common rooms and hallways of the seminary in as a discrete manner as possible. He observed his fellow students just as discretely, but without any obvious evidence coming to hand.

In his cell he sat and thought about the events of the previous days. Back at his Parish church in Santiago, Father Leon had taught him a way to recall the small details which were often ignored during such a general investigation. He sat on his bed, closed his eyes and relaxed his body by imagining his muscles as being twisted rope. From the toes upward, he imagined these ropes slowly untwisting until those of his neck and face were once more limp strands. Then he put all of his daily thoughts out of his mind by slowly repeating over and over in his mind the first part of the 'Hail Mary':

"Ave Maria, gratia plena, Dominus tecum".[3]

[3] *In Latin, this is: "Ave Maria, gratia plena, Dominus tecum. Or in English: "Hail Mary, full of grace, the Lord is with Thee.*

Then he would recall the past events which came to him as a vision. He saw the visitors arriving through the open gates of the seminary and meeting their friends and loved ones in the outer courtyard which had been decorated with garlands of flowers, flags and holy banners. There were tables of food and drink, and the guests were talking to their sponsors. He saw his friends Antonio and Felipe laughing together and sharing drinks with their invited friends; he saw Antonio Navarro in animated conversation with a beautiful girl. Stop! This was very unusual for Navarro to show much emotion to anyone, and especially to a young woman. He had often decried the value of women and now he was laughing and freely speaking with this beautiful young girl.

Matteo concentrated and let his mind gather its thoughts about the incongruous couple. The girl was obviously younger than Navarro. There were some similarities in her stance and mannerisms, but she was not of European descent but rather had the lovely completion, black hair and high cheekbones of an Andina. His sister perhaps?

Then in his mind Matteo saw the girl offer Navarro a goblet of wine. He deliberately poured a little onto the ground and then drank from it. This was a custom well-known to Matteo. It was considered to be good manners within Andino society to offer a small amount of food and drink to Pachamama, the ancient Incan goddess of the Earth and protector of children.

Then Matteo's mind wandered, still thinking about Antonio Navarro. There was something else about him which Matteo had observed briefly and passed over without a moment's thought. What was it? Yes, he remembered now! There was Navarro sitting opposite him at the evening meal not long after the robbery. He reached across to take some bread from the central bowl and whilst his hands had been scrubbed clean, there were slight traces of brown clay beneath his fingernails, evidence that he had been working in the pottery section of the seminary's recreation room.

Matteo suddenly opened his eyes and sat bolt upright. He now knew where the golden chalice had been taken and why it had not been found even after a thorough search of every room in the seminary. He got up and rushed out of his cell and along the balcony in search of brother Antonio. He knocked at his cell door and there was no answer so he went to the library where most of his fellow students would be at this time of day, reading or discussing some aspects of their previous lessons. He was not there also.

Downstairs, Matteo looked into many of the small recesses and in the garden of the inner courtyard where students often went for solitude. Nothing.

Walking through the archway which connected the two courtyards, Matteo saw that the chapel door was open. He went in and in its dim light, lit only by a small lamp at the altar, he saw a lone figure at prayer in one of the forward pews. It was Navarro.

Matteo entered and quietly walked down the aisle and when he was a few paces from where Navarro was praying, he softly spoke a common saying in Mapudungun, the language of the Mapuche People and still spoken in many parts of Chile, especially near Santiago. "Ñuke pu zomo, wenüy negün küzaw, püle iñchiñ ñi wñamün Ñuke Mapu[4]".

Without thinking, Navarro instinctively replied with the usual affirmation to this saying in the same language:

"Ñiñel mapu, nien zungun, ¡Ñi pu che ruka!"[5].

[4] *Translated from the Mapudungun language of the Mapuche people: "You can come near to God if you make friends with people who love God"*
[5] *From the Mapudungun: "And what good friends we've come to be!"*

Suddenly realising what he had said, Navarro looked up in fright as Matteo knelt down beside him and put one arm around his shoulders and quietly said:

"Your cross is too heavy to bear alone, Brother Antonio. I know about the chalice and wish to help you. Come! Let us go back to your cell as I believe that all of the answers are to be had there. Navarro looked at Matteo and he had tears in his eyes; his head now slumped down onto his chest as he slowly stood up. The two men walked slowly out of the chapel, Matteo's arm still around the other man's shoulders. At the door, Matteo took his arm away and the two seminarians walked together up the stairs and to Navarro's cell.

They went in and Navarro sat on his bed, his eyes downcast and his hands nervously clasping together in his lap. As he suspected, there was an earthenware chalice containing a variety of pens sitting on the desk below the window. It had been crudely fashioned and some of the decoration was incomplete. It had been made in a hurry.

Matteo went over and picked it up. It was much too heavy for a simple earthenware chalice, so he tipped out the pens and began to lightly tap the chalice on the side of the desk much like one would lightly tap the shell of a hard-boiled egg on the side of a pot. Small cracks appeared in the earthenware and Matteo used his finger and thumb to peel off the hardened flacks of the pottery shell. The bright flash of gold shone in the sunlight streaming through the window. The golden chalice had been found!

Matteo completed his task and swept the broken pieces of pottery into the pocket of his soutane[6]. He turned to Navarro and stretched out his hand which was holding the chalice.

"It is now your task, Brother Antonio to undo the wrong which you have done. God is merciful and you will be forgiven, but only you

[6] Robe

can return this chalice whilst the chapel is empty".

Navarro took the chalice and looked up at Matteo: "How did you know it was me?" he asked in a faint voice.

Matteo sat down on the bed next to his friend and quietly revealed how he had come to the conclusion as to who was the thief and where he had taken the chalice.

"Firstly, you have been much too vocal about the nobility of your family and the lack of worth of the local people. Secondly, I suspected that you were not what you claimed, and this was confirmed when I saw you talking to that beautiful girl when our guests were here. Is she your sister?"

"My half-sister." Navarro replied.

"Next, there was the offering to Pachamama. Only one who respects the old customs of the Andino would have done such a thing. You are, like me, a mestizo – of mixed Spanish and local blood, I assume?"

"Yes." Navarro replied. Matteo noticed that now he sat more upright and looked more relaxed. He continued.

"Yes, Brother Matteo. I stole the chalice as it was a symbol to me of an oppressive time in our country's history; a time when the Spaniards, represented by my family, oppressed the common people. I am indeed the son of Hector Navarro Torres, descendent of proud Conquistadores, but also the offspring of one of his servants, my mother Maria. She was cast out of the Navarro household and when I was born, I was raised by my mother in her village of Santa Cruz which is not far from here. The young woman that you saw was indeed my younger sister, Luciana. My father did, however, have some feelings of guilt towards my mother, so he sent money for my upbringing and education. Luckily, I was a good scholar and had also served in the local church where Father Sebastián gave me more encouragement to serve God. With my father's influence and the good Father's recommendation, I secured a position here at the seminary. Can you understand what torment I have had in my life, Matteo?

"Yes, my friend. As a mestizo I too have had some difficulty in my family, and now, like yourself seek to be of some service to God. Come, it is time for you to return the chalice. I will come with you as far as the chapel to see that it is unoccupied. Then I will leave you to do what is right and to your own conscience about what you make of your future."

The two men returned to the chapel doors. Matteo quickly looked in and motioned Navarro to enter. He then closed the door and returned to his own cell, confident that his friend would find repentance.

It was to everyone's surprise that the golden chalice had returned to its place of honour; everyone except Matteo and Navarro. A prayer was said for its return and forgiveness for the one who had taken it.

A week later, Antonio Navarro Torres quietly left the seminary. The night before, he had quietly come to Matteo's cell and thanked him for his help in regaining his peace and his soul. Then he left just as quietly.

It was after the morning prayers the next day when Father Lorenzo caught up to Matteo as he walked back to his cell to prepare for breakfast.

"Thank you, Matteo for what you did for Brother Antonio and San Isidro. The Rector told me that he had gone to him to give his confession and also told him of your part in the return of the golden chalice. That was certainly a very interesting piece of deductive reasoning which went beyond the investigative powers of the rest of us – and the local Prefecture, I must add."

"Brother Antonio needed help, and I was able to give it. That's all, Father." Matteo said quietly. "What will become of him?"

Father Lorenzo looked at him and smiled:
"What are the three moral virtues of the old Incan religion? Ama Sua; Ama Llulla; and Ama Quella[7] are they not?"

Matteo looked at his mentor with some surprise. "Our Brother Antonio," he continued, "will go back to his Parish at Santiago with a simple letter from the Rector that the life of our order was not suited for him and with a recommendation that he follow the path of another order which has fewer demands. Nothing more will be said of it here. Do you agree, Brother Matteo?"

Matteo smiled and quietly said, "Thank you Father Lorenzo, that is for the best for I truly

---

[7] *Ama Sua (do not be a thief), Ama Llulla (do not be a liar) and Ama Quella (do not be idle).*

believe that Antonio Navarro is now a better man, and the story of the missing golden chalice is now at an end. Amen"

Story Ten

Of Pumas and Frogs
(De Pumas y Ranas)

This is a story about Puno, the city which sits on the central and western side of Lake Titicaca in Peru and some of its legends.

My servant Alfredo and I alighted from our carriage of the newly built rail line connecting Cuzco with Puno in southern Peru. We walked through the platform gates and hired a small donkey trap which would take us to our posada[1] on the avenida La Torre, one of the main streets of Puno[2], only a few blocks away. It was dark by then, so we appreciated the cheerful lights of the posada's courtyard as well as the welcome by its owner, Señor Braulio, an

[1] *A family inn common to many South American countries.*
[2] *Puno (Aymara and Quechua: Punu) is a city in south-eastern Peru, located on the shore of Lake Titicaca. It is the capital city of Puno Province and was established in 1668 by viceroy Pedro Antonio Fernández de Castro.*

open and friendly man who seemed to have a solution to every problem.

The next day, I made arrangements to visit the Head of the Philosophy Department at the Universidad de Puno; my reason for making the journey to Puno. Alfredo had alternatively decided to visit the well-known and popular Mercado de Contrabando[3] at the waterfront. Señor Braulio had told him about these markets over many glasses of cerveza[4] the previous night so he was interested in seeing what small items he could buy having the extra excitement that they were illegal goods. Old soldiers are like that.

These markets were extensive and sold about everything imaginable from food items to the latest household items. There had always been an active trading network across Lake Titicaca from one side to the other; well before the Incas and then the Spaniards arrived. The Spaniards

[3] *Contraband market where smuggled goods are sold.*
[4] *Beer*

had carved up the country into their many and separate governmental regions with little regard to the tribal boundaries of the indigenous people. The border between southern Peru and Bolivia was thus arbitrarily drawn down through Lake Titicaca. But the trading network across the lake continued. To be sure, both counties maintained small naval units to control smuggling, but the outcome was never in doubt. It would be hard for Customs Officers to arrest people who were their relatives and perhaps they too also gained from some trading. Who knows? Whenever government officials arrived from Lima or Cuzco, there naturally would be some arrests. Juan, or Pedro or Antonio would be seized and locked up for the duration of the official's inspection and then released thereafter. The Mercado de Contrabando thrived, especially with woollen goods made in the homes of both countries.

For my part, I walked down towards the lake and to the Universidad de Puno to pay my respects to the Head of Philosophy there.

Professor Guillermo Roberto Rojas was a rotund, gregarious man of about fifty years of age. He greeted me with a firm handshake and a broad smile.

"Welcome to Puno, Doctor Moreno. I hope that you would stay a while with us. I have read some of your papers and I am interested in your work on the soldier-philosophers of ancient Greece."

"Thank you, Don Guillermo, but alas my visit will be but a short one. I am continuing my journey to La Paz where I also have some research tasks," I replied.

"Well in that case, Doctor Moreno, allow me to show you a little of our city. Come! I hope that you do not mind walking as that is the best way to see our city?" With that he picked up his hat from his desk and walked briskly out of his study. I followed as fast as I could to keep up with his fast pace.

We walked around the edge of the lake along the avenida Costanera with its open park on one side and the broad waters of Lake Titicaca on the other. The buildings along this avenue were the usual adobe structures of two or three storeys that seemed to be occupied by traders in the most part. We turned into a broad street, the calle Los Incas, which led into the heart of the city.

The people who went about their daily tasks seemed healthy enough; some in modern European dress, others in local costumes and others in a more colourful mixture of both. The dress was usually sober in the main with men in trousers, shirts and sandals and the ladies in long skirts and colourful lliclas[5] and a variety of head wear denoting their village of origin; the small bowler hats, recently imported for the railway workers were most common.

---

[5] *Llicllas (pronounced Yeek-ya) — The* lliclla *or* manta *is a colourful cape worn by Quechua women, woven in the shape of a square and worn across the back and shoulders like a miniature shawl.*

We crossed several main streets and then continued walking along to where the calle Los Incas suddenly narrowed until it opened into a small plaza. To our right was an impressive stone building painted blue with white simulated colonnades and white balconies on its line of windows.

"You like our beautiful building?" asked the professor seeing my interest.

"Yes, it is a most impressive" I replied.

"It is the Glorioso Colegio Nacional de San Antonio[6] that was founded in 1828 by the great liberator Simon Bolivar himself. It is one of our most prestigious educational institutions here, dedicated to our young people. Its' most famous son was Manuel Pino who was also a teacher of philosophy here. During the war with the

[6] *Glorious National College of Saint Charles. Saint Charles or San Carlos, was Charles Borromeo (Italian:1538 – 1584) was the Latin archbishop of Milan and a cardinal of the Catholic Church who carried out many reforms.*

Chileans, he and his students fought them when this very square was made into one of the Chilean's barracks. Unfortunately, he later died at the Battle of Miraflores[7]. The good citizens of Puno have plans to name this square after him and to build a statue in his honour. Were you in the war, Doctor Morano?" he asked.

"I was just a Reservist." I replied. "No great battles for me, I am afraid. Regretfully, I spent most of my time at the university recruiting poor young students to be soldiers."

"Well, then. Let us not talk of such sad events for that was a time in our history which was most regrettable. Here is the Church of San Juan Bautista," he said, pointing to a lovely church opposite the college. It had three frontal spires and was painted in white, yellow and grey.

"It has recently been rebuilt on the site of the old chapel which probably predated the

[7] *The Battle of Miraflores occurred on January 15, 1881 in the Miraflores District of Lima.*

founding of this city in 1668. It may be only a small church, but it is very important church to the people in this city because it holds the statue of the Virgen of Candelaria[8] - the patron saint of Puno".

I felt the urge to go in and look at the adored statue of the Virgin, but perhaps another time. Professor Guillermo quickly walked off, turning into a narrow, cobbled street which contained many small shops huddled together in the usual style and usually of two-storey adobe brick with red tiled rooves. Soon we entered the main plaza.

"Here is our Plaza de Armas where you can see the usual government buildings, the police barracks, and of course our beautiful cathedral,

[8] *Originally from an appearance in Tenerife, in the Canary Islands, of the Virgin carrying a candle in one hand and the baby Jesus in the other. She is venerated in many countries. In Puno, from January 24 to February 11, a festival is celebrated in homage to her and is a mixture of both Catholic, and the pre-Hispanic religions with the Virgin of Candelaria being strongly associated with the Pachamama or 'Mother Earth' of the Incas.*

the Catedral Basílica San Antonio Borromeo. It was built in the Andean Baroque style and finished in 1747. Let's push on, but you must visit the cathedral before you leave."

We walked past the ordered stone walls of the cathedral and along the jirón[9] Deustua which suddenly became very steep as we climbed up into the side of the wide amphitheatre which holds the city against the wide stretch of the blue Lake Titicaca.

It was a very difficult climb, even for one used to the high altitude of the Altiplano, but eventually we reached a small, flat rocky knoll upon which was built a wide stone plinth in the Incan style showing a broad, square face. Surmounting this was a stature of an Inca dressed in the traditional kilt and robe of a chief. His stern face looking out towards the lake.

[9] *Jirón — a small, narrow street named after Alejandro Octavio Deustua Escarza (1849 - 1945), a Peruvian philosopher, educator, statesman and Prime Minister of Peru from 9 August 1902 until 4 November 1902.*

"This is the cerrito Huajsapata[10] and the statue is of Manco Cápac, the founder of the Inca Empire. It is said that he and his family were born on an island in the lake, the children of Inti the god of the Sun. But I am sure that you know that story well?" he said with a knowing look.

"Indeed," I answered with a smile. "My mother, whose ancestors were of the Incan nobility of Cuzco often told me the story"

"Ah! But did you know that there are supposed to be great caves and tunnels under this hill which reach all the way to the Temple of the Sun[11] in your fair city?"

[10] *Cerrito = little hill and the indigenous word 'Huajsapata' pronounced 'hhrrr sapata' and is often given a meaning of 'witness of my love' so it probably refers to the love of the Lake and the land by the Inca Manco Cápac or simply a 'lovers' hill' with a beautiful view of the lake.*
[11] *Templo de Koricancha   - 'The Golden Temple', from the Quechua 'quri' for gold and' kancha' for an enclosure. Also called the Temple of the Sun it was the original Incan. The Convent of Santo Domingo, the monastery of the Dominicans was built upon it in 1680.*

"No!" I laughed, "that is one story which my mother neglected to tell me. Perhaps one day we could find them and use them as a fast way of travelling between the two cities."

He turned and faced the vast extent of the lake which stretched out before us beyond the terracotta rooves of the city. It was a fine day and I could see the distant hills stretching out on either side of the blue waters of the lake, merging with the sky and white clouds in the distance.

"You see that knoll higher up on the surrounding ridge?" the professor continued. "That is called the Mirador Puma Uta[12] and from there we would get a much better understanding of the immensity of this great lake before us. It is said that the name of the lake comes from the local Aymara word 'Titiq'aq'a' which loosely translates as the 'grey puma'. There is much debate about this and why the name should refer to our wild cat. Some say this

12 *The Lookout of the Sacred Puma.*

refers to an ancient carving of a puma on the side of the sacred island of Isla del Sol out there on the lake, but others say that it refers to the very shape of the lake itself which looks like a hunting puma. The Incas believed the puma, condor and the snake to be sacred because of its respective strength, ability to fly and its speed. But who knows?"

I looked out again at the sparkling blue waters of this, the highest of deep freshwater lakes and imagined how the ancient inhabitants could imagine the shape of this lake as a great puma as seen from above, but then I remembered the stone outlines of animals on the coastal plain of Nazca well to our north. It was well within the mathematical and surveying knowledge of these ancient people to visualise a surface feature from above.

"There is another local story about the lake and another one of its creatures which I find fascinating." the professor said. He sat down on the rock with his back against the statue's plinth and wiped his brow with an old handkerchief. "Would you like to hear it?"

"To be sure, Professor, I know little of the local stories hereabouts, as my people came from Cuzco well after the Incas settled there." I replied, joining the old man on sharp, grey stone.

"Good! Well then, let me begin" he said as he straightened out his shirt front much as I imagined he would do at the start of one of his lectures at the university.

"It is a story of a toad," he laughed, "or more correctly, a frog. *Telmatobius culeus*, to be exact; commonly known as the Titicaca Water Frog. It is a medium to large frog which inhabits the lake but is becoming very scarce in recent times. It is said that they once occurred here in very large numbers and that they inhabited a fabulous city beneath the lake. The story goes on to say that one night, when the Incan army of

Túpac Yupanqui[13] arrived at the lake not far from the sacred site of Puma Uta, one of the night sentries encountered a beautiful woman dressed in a wide, flowing green robe who had large, golden eyes which spoke to him of love. He became bewitched by her and fell into a happy, deep sleep. When he was awoken by the relieving guard, he was ashamed and told him about the beautiful young maiden with the golden eyes. Alarmed at this, the rest of the guard was called out and the men searched the totora reeds around the shores of the lake. There they encountered this beautiful maiden with the golden eyes. When they pursued her, she was suddenly transformed into a giant frog with golden eyes and after taking one last look at the men, dived into the smooth, dark waters of the lake. When the Inca[14] heard of this, he had his men cast great nets into the water. When they

[13] Túpac Yupanqui *1441–c. 1493, the son of Pachacuti, was the tenth Inca of the Inca Empire and his son was Huayna Capac.*
[14] *The term 'Inca' refers to the emperor here as well as to his people.*

hauled them in, they were full of a great number of frogs led by two of great size with green skin and large golden eyes. In front of the Inca, the two great frogs turned into the beautiful woman and her equally handsome consort. They gave the Inca a haughty glance and then returned to their natural shape, leading their companions out of the lake and up into the hills beyond the astonished soldiers. Inti the sun had just appeared over the mountains to the east and seeing the plight of frogs who were now in danger from the spears of the soldiers, turned them into the large stones you can see not far from here."

I looked up towards the ridge of the Puma Uta just above us and around the statue were large, rounded stones and I could now imagine a group of frogs fleeing up the steep hill from the spears of the Incan soldiers.

"Furthermore" continued the professor, "it is said that some of the locals still believe that there is a mysterious city beneath the lake, and, should you go to the shore at midnight and encounter one of its inhabitants, they will offer you ears of corn made of gold for the return of their king and queen. A fascinating story is it not?"

"Yes indeed, Professor. The lake certainly looks as though it would contain great mystery , and it is interesting how all local peoples have tales which explain their natural surroundings."

My thoughts were suddenly interrupted when my eye caught a smudge of faint black smoke well out upon the water. "Professor, there is a steamer out on the lake!" I exclaimed.

"You have good eyes, Doctor Moreno, that is indeed a steamer. It is our *Yavari* which is both a gunboat for our navy and a cargo boat which carries passengers across the lake. It was named after the Yavary[15] River, a tributary of the Amazon on our north-eastern border with Brazil."

[15] *Also called the Javary River.*

"But where was it built?" I enquired, "I know of no shipyard anywhere near the lake!"

"Ah, that is the beauty of our industrial age, Doctor Moreno. The *Yavari* was built in an ironworks in London in 1861 and then broken down into small pieces which could be reassembled. It was shipped out to Arica on what was once the coast of Bolivia, then by railway to Tacna and then on the backs of poor mules up the mountain roads here to the lake where it was reassembled. Quite a feat of engineering, yes?"

"That is a remarkable story, Professor, but where does the *Yavari* get its fuel; its coal, its timber?"

"Ah. Yes, more of the adaptability and common sense of Peru! The *Yavari* is able to use dried llama dung as its fuel. We are an ingenious people and there are plenty of llamas here in the Altiplano." He said, tapping the side of his nose with his finger. "It combines the unusual functions of a gunboat, a passenger ship and of course a trading vessel – but I doubt that there is much use for it as a gunboat. We are usually on good terms with our Bolivian neighbours across the lake and the smuggling trade between the two countries is almost an acceptable occupation. The local people were trading across the lake for centuries before the Spaniards decided to draw a border line down its middle."

I looked out across the broad, blue waters of the lake and the hills beyond. There was a momentary flash of light closer into the city on a broad expanse of yellow floating on the water.

"What is over there?" I asked and pointed in the direction of the expanse of yellow.

"Ha!" said the professor, "you have found the home of Los Uros[16] who live on the floating islands made from tied bundles of the totora reed found in abundance around the lake. It is said that they fled to the lake to escape invaders.

[16] *Uru or Los Uros (Qhas Qut suñi in the old Uru language).*

Perhaps the Aymara who lived here and certainly the Incas and Spaniards who came later. They build beautiful boats of reed bundles and live in comfortable reed thatched houses on their many islands. Of course, they are now very much assimilated with the mainland peoples but many still prefer their island homes and their own way of life."

"How do they make a living?" I asked, "fishing perhaps?"

"Oh, yes. They are good fishermen, and they make small fish pens by cutting a large square hole in their islands which they then line with nets. They catch the fish from the lake and then put them into their pens where they breed them and have fish whenever they want. Clever? No?"

"They would seem to have a good life then?" I replied.

"Well, most of the time. Their fears of the mainlanders have long since disappeared as has their language and customs and many have moved ashore over time. There is one interesting family tradition which remains when they need to maintain peace and harmony."

"Yes, what is that?" I asked.

"Well, now! if one member of the family has a major falling out or has dishonoured the family group, they simply cut off the part of the island occupied by the offender's home with the large saws they use to shape their island. The offender is allowed to drift away from the family group to start a new life. Of course, should a new member join the family, it is an easy task to weave more reeds together and form a new part of the island for more living space."

The professor continued his description of the sights and history of the city of Puno. He was very proud of the city and of its potential for the future.

"There has been a great variation in the fortunes of Puno, especially with the demise of the silver mines to the east and the slump in the alpaca wool trade caused by the recent war[17], but we have the railway to Arequipa and beyond to the coast, so trade is beginning to return."

With that comment, he turned and made his way down the sharp limestone rocks of the cerrito. I followed and we walked back down the hill and into the street which ran next to the eastern side of the cathedral. We stopped at a small, rectangular archway with a tiled roof next to a neat, two-storeyed building painted in a bright yellow colour. A small sign on the wall next to the archway read 'Café Bar' where the professor bade me enter.

[17] *The War of the Pacific (1879 to 1884) – Chile annexed the coastal strip of Bolivia, south of Peru which was an important trade routes for these two countries. Bolivia and Peru went to war with Chile and lost and now the coastal centres form part of Chile.*

Through the archway was a small but delightful tiled courtyard filled with a variety of flowering cactus plants and wooden seats and tables. Beyond was the welcoming interior of the café.

"Time for a good coffee, if you would like one, Doctor Moreno, or perhaps something more traditional such as mate de coca[18] should you need it, " he said with a sideways glance and a smile.

I laughed at that suggestion. "Thank you, all the same, but as a native of Cuzco I know the use of coca very well and I am well at home at this altitude."

"Perhaps it is not too early for you to try our local drink in honour of the hill we have just climbed – the *Huajsapata*[19]. It is a hot mulled

---

[18] *An herbal tea made by infusing leaves of the coca plant in boiling water. Very useful for altitude sickness.*
[19] *This is a hot mulled wine mixed with grenadine, orange bitters and spices served with a slice of orange. Pisco, a form of Peruvian brandy is a much better substitute for the wine.*

wine which you can only find here in Puno. Too much of it in our cold winter at this altitude will give you altitude sickness even if you are an Andino," he laughed as we entered the café. "Come! Let us have a good coffee and then I will show you our beautiful cathedral before I let you go in our faculty library."

Story Eleven

The Virgin of Copacabana
(La Virgen de Copacabana)

This is another story from Bolivia and from the region of Lake Titicaca. It is also another about the faith of the people who live there.

The next morning, after a very restful night in a comfortable bed, Julio my colleague and I went downstairs for breakfast. It was a simple affair, as was usual in these parts; warm bread rolls with jam, fresh fruit and sweetened coffee. There was even the option of a fried egg which I declined.

The coach to take us from Peru and on to La Paz in neighbouring Bolivia had already been loaded with our baggage. I noted that the passengers who had already taken their seats up on top of coach now looked forward in anticipation for our departure. They were local people who travelled in the hope to sell their wares; traders with baskets of fruit and small hand-made goods going on to the next village.

There were the usual pleasantries as our fellow travellers inside the coach again resumed their seats. One austere-looking gentleman of more than middle age looked like a rather disgruntled undertaker. He gave us a gruff '¡Buenos días!' and pushed in ahead, going straight to the far window seat without any ceremony. This was much to the disgust of two other passengers, an Englishman and his portly wife, who had showed some distaste at having to wait their turn to enter the coach. His wife bustled up into the cabin, finding her many skirts and hand luggage to be of some hindrance. Her husband attempted to assist by giving her a gentle push from behind before heavily climbing aboard with considerable expenditure of breath. Julio and I followed and then the young man, who seemed to be a student, nimbly took his seat with a shy smile as though he had been caught out missing lectures.

There is something about beginning a journey early in the morning; people are still recovering from the previous evening's revels or still in that level of consciousness which sleep has yet to relinquish.

Today, according to our coachman, we would be again travelling around the borders of the lake but now heading more to the east towards the border with Bolivia only fifty kilometres away. There would be a stop and change of horses at the border of course and then on to Copacabana. The coach would then go on to the lake crossing at San Pedro de Tiquina for the night before making the crossing of the narrow strait by punt the next day.

The countryside did not change that much although there seemed to be a few more trees, widely spaced, along the dusty road. They gave some comfort in the usual barren nature of the low hills and rocky outcrops which seem to be the usual landscape around this part of the lake. The small farmhouses of thatched adobe and the many fields separated by rock walls continued.

People, both men and women trudged along the side of the road; some carrying bundles on their backs or walking behind their small burros overladen with produce or firewood, a scarce commodity in these parts.

We passed through the small village of Yunguyo which was not far from the border. Its many small houses and shops were huddled close together in the bright, thin air of the new day along the dusty road. Some of the shop owners were beginning to open their broad shutters to display their merchandise and some customers lounged against the walls waiting for other shops to open. The few dogs in the street also waited patiently.

Eventually the coach stopped next to a small inn which was open with its owner standing in the street beckoning us all to come into his shop for refreshment. The dusty travellers from the upper seats climbed down and opened their own earthenware flasks of water or chicha, the corn beer so popular in these mountains and small packages containing corn, potatoes, tamales and some dried meat.

It was too early for my own lunch, but Julio, being of a practical nature, had brought with him a small package containing bread and some sangrecita[1] left over from our breakfast. The Undertaker had remained outside, and the student had purchased a small flask of local juice. The Englishman had taken my advice and had ordered two cups of mate de coca to assist with his adjustment to the thin air of this altitude as well as for his mid-morning refreshment. The tea was naturally served in rough, earthenware mugs rather than the chinaware which his wife had expected. She delicately tasted the beverage and pulled a face of disgust and handed the mug back to her husband.

[1] *Sangrecita is a blood sausage made from chicken blood, seasoned with garlic, onion, chili pepper, herbs and often prepared with baked potatoes, fried sweet potatoes or cassava.*

"Perhaps the Señora would prefer one of our excellent local fruit juices? "I suggested to her husband who now stood with two mugs of mate and a look of uncertainty on his face. He brightened up at my suggestion and I turned to the owner and said in Spanish:

"I am sorry; the mate is not to the Señora's taste. Could she have some jugo[2] please?"

The owner soon returned with a glass of fresh juice which the 'good lady wife' tasted suspiciously at first and then drank with some relish. Her husband was most pleased, and she also voiced a quite 'thank you' to me in appreciation.

To the horror of the Englishman, the coach then departed without its passengers. He stood open-mouthed and with his hand up pointing in a gesture of bewilderment after the receding coach.

[2] *Jugo is fruit juice, often made from pulverising fresh fruit, it is more like a Western 'smoothie'.*

"Do not worry, Señor," I said "the coach is merely going on to the Bolivian customs office on the other side of the border. The coachman has completed all of the necessary formalities with our customs officers here and we must do that also. You see? Our customs office is just across the road."

I pointed to the small white building across the dusty street where the sign over the arched doorway read 'Control Migratorio Peru'.

"After that, I am afraid we will have to walk up the hill then cross the border by foot. It is only a short way, and after some more formalities we will again board our coach."

The Englishman and his wife had not expected to walk today and made the short journey up the hill with some difficulty. Julio, being an honourable man, had taken up the lady's small travelling bag with a gentle 'permítame, Señora' and helped her and her husband up the road and under the broad, stone archway which was decorated with a faded sign which read 'Bienvenido a Bolivia[3].

The formalities with the Bolivian Custom's Officers were friendly and over quickly. Our travel documents, being complete had passed inspection without any enquiry. The Englishman and his wife were questioned briefly about their intensions in La Paz, and I was able to act as translator, so they too passed inspection.

Our coach was parked outside, where the horses were stamping their feet and nodding their heads ready to go. Everyone clambered aboard, pleased with themselves that there had been little delay at this border crossing, and so we commenced our journey towards Copacabana. Just up the hill, a road marker indicated that it was just eleven kilometres away and soon the coach was rattling its way down the hill which led into the city.

---

[3] *'Welcome to Bolivia'*

As the coach rattled down the hill towards the city, my first impressions of Copacabana were very favourable. The city was nestled between several hills around a single broad bay, where the waters of Lake Titicaca were a sparkling blue in the midday sun. For the most part, the houses were of two or even three stories, painted in a variety of bright colours and most were roofed with dark red tiles. The streets were narrow as was typical of most towns in the Andes with people going about their business dress in a variety of mixed local and European garb. My almanac informed me that the good people of Copacabana were mostly of the Aymara people, as at Puno in Peru; the Spanish simply drawing a border through the lake to mark their own personal political territory with little regard to natural or local indigenous boundaries. It was the same all over this continent as peoples and often families became separated into different national populations.

Our coach stopped at a small yard within the city not far from the waterfront. This and its adjacent building acted as the coaching station.

The passengers on top of the cab soon gathered up their bundles and quickly merged into the small crowd which had gathered to meet the coach; some to greet the newcomers, others to await their turn to board the coach for its departure for the overnight stop at San Pablo de Tiquina, further towards La Paz.

Our fellow travellers from the cab alighted and stood around adjusting their clothing or taking their baggage which was being handed down from the roof of the cabin by the assistant driver. The Undertaker, we noted with some interest, took his small bag and quickly disappeared into the crowd. The student gave us a shy smile and faint wave of goodbye and went into the building to wait being called for on the next leg of his journey. The Englishman, now occupied with his wife's fussy concerns being in a new place surrounded by foreigners, looked over and gave us a nod of farewell and then they joined the student.

I had taken the trouble to telegraph ahead from Cuzco to book into an hotel which had been recommended to me by the owner of our posada in Puno and we looked around for a representative from it. A little way from the coach stood a tired-looking old man dressed in drab European working clothes and standing next to a small pushcart. He was holding a small sign with my name roughly chalked upon it, I quickly walked over to him and identified myself, motioning to Julio to join me. We placed our small bags near the cart

The porter went to the elaborate ritual of loading our small luggage on board his handcart and with a beckoning arm led us up a small, cobbled lane towards the large hill which dominated the eastern side of the city.

"That is the cerro Calvario[4]," he said, pointing up to the top of the hill, "it is an important site for the pilgrimage. You have come for this perhaps, Señores?" He asked, grunting under the strain of pushing his cart which was only partially occupied by our meagre luggage.

[4] *Calvary Hill*

"No, my friend, we are just simple travellers here on business. We have yet to explore your lovely city." I replied.

With that he brightened up and stood more erect, now pleased that he now could be the tour guide rather than a lowly porter. He put down the handle of the pushcart and pointed up to the summit of the rocky crag which was above us.

"Why, Señores, that is a most important place here in Copa. It is said that up there is the spot where, in 1697 a poor man with bad eyesight came across a mysterious llama which then spat into his eye as these animals often do when startled. From that moment he was able to see with extraordinary clarity. This miracle made his vision became so impressive that he was the envy of all the local people who then created a replica of the fourteen Stations of the Cross on top of that very hill."

Having told his story, our guide bent over and picked up the handles of his cart and continued his laborious journey up the cobbled lane. Soon we came out onto a wide street which traversed the hill. On the corner with it and our lane, stood an imposing three-story building made from whitewashed stone, with several tall glass windows facing the road.

The words 'Hotel Nueva España[5]" were proudly written in red on a yellow board which jutted out from the corner of the structure. The entrance was by way of a double glass door through which the porter pushed as he ushered us inside.

Whilst this was clearly a colonial-era building, it was obvious that the old Spanish style had been greatly modified. The entrance archway with the usual double wooden doors had been replaced by attractive, modern double glass-panelled doors which opened into a narrow foyer with a side door which led into a well-lit dining room. On the other side of the foyer was an office and front desk. This foyer opened out

[5] *Hotel New Spain*

into a wide, spacious area which would have been the interior courtyard of an older Spanish house. However, whilst it retained the surrounding upper galleries off which the rooms were entered, the courtyard was not completely open to the sky. There was a roof made of beams raising to a central point in its crown. There were many skylights around the edges of the roof made of framed yellow glass which gave the entire interior a cheerful, sunny glow. The central fountain was still there but the usual gardens had been replaced by many potted plants, mainly of the cacti variety and the rest of the floor was painted in dark green and covered here and there with rugs decorated in the Incan style. Several tapestries depicting local motifs hung from the walls on the ground floor which, like their old Spanish counterparts contained a few doors but no windows.

A jovial man with a broad smiling face emerged from behind the foyer's counter. "Greetings, Señores! welcome to 'The Nueva España'. I am Señor Robles your host."

"Thank you, Señor Robles. This is my colleague Señor Lorca." I said using Julio's family name. "We should be staying here for a few days."

Señor Robles smiled and said, "Meanwhile, let me take you to your rooms. Manuel will bring up your bags."

Walking into the spacious courtyard he swept his arm around and said with a smile of pride. "This is our grand foyer should you wish to rest. There is a table with fruit which we put out each day and a jar of coca leaves should you wish to partake. There is always water boiling in our kitchen from which the Night Manager would be happy to provide you with should you need mate de coca in the night."

I smiled at this courtesy often given to guests who have trouble with the altitude. "Thank you, Señor Robles, but my friend and I come from Cuzco and are both suited to these heights, but we do enjoy mate de coca, never-the-less."

"A-ha!" he laughed, "then we will see you in our lovely dining room for mate de coca with our complimentary breakfast starting at six," he said, pointing through another double set of glass doors which opened into the grand foyer. We thanked him for his courtesy and followed Manuel who was now walking up the stairs to our rooms on the second floor. He had indicated that the bathroom was just a few doors along at the corner of the landing as he opened the door to our room. Here we found our room to be simply but tastefully furnished with two comfortable beds and adequate hanging spaces for our clothing. An old-fashioned mahogany and marble-topped washstand with its large white porcelain pitcher and basin stood below a large mirror fixed to the wall. I gave Manuel a few extra coins for his hard work and introduction to his lovely city. He touched his forehead and gave us a huge grin.

"Many thanks, Señores, I am to be found at the door behind the small desk in the far corner of the grand foyer should you ever require my humble services," he said and quietly closed the door as he left.

Having settled our things in our room, Julio and I went downstairs and out onto the street. The hotel had been built high up on the hill, so we had a commanding view of the city. The overall view was one of orderliness with many brightly coloured buildings, and several long streets running down from the rugged hills behind the city to the sparkling waterfront on the lake. Here there were clusters of small boats and several long jetties reaching out into the water. Over on the far side of the city was a large cathedral of imposing size, painted uniformly in white, with several copper domes and a tower of several spires.

We walked down the hill through the small, cobbled lane up which we had come with Manuel. There was a storm developing across the lake which was known for its turbulence during such times. The sky had become very dark, save for a fiery red glow which shone like an angry eye just above the hills to the west. A sudden bright flash of lightning hit the water some way off from the shore so Julio and I hurried for shelter. We walked quickly down into the calle Santivañez[6] where we found a small café. Later, having partaken of a good meal and some of the local wine, we returned to the hotel for a good night's rest thankful that there would be no more coach travelling the next day.

That day being a Sunday, Julio and I decided to go to Mass in the impressive cathedral that stood on one side of the city. At his desk, Señor Robles was in a talkative mood and very proud of his city, told us that the beautiful cathedral down the hill and across the plaza was called the Basilica of Our Lady of Copacabana, and it housed the statue of the Virgen de Copacabana, the patron saint of all Bolivia. He had also said that it had been constructed on the site of an earlier Augustine chapel, itself being built on the original temple sacred to the Incas. The

[6] *Santivañez Street, named after the city in central Bolivia.*

Basilica itself began many years later in 1668 but was not completed until 1805.

It was a fine, sunny day and the lake sparkled in the early sunlight; Inti the sun smiled on Copacabana that morning.

Walking up to the main plaza, we passed many small street stalls. Here the ladies of Copacabana, many in their wide skirts, brightly coloured shawls and bowler hats sold a variety of produce. These included a vast array of nuts, fruit, sweets, small jugs of chicha and flower petals of many colours. I was intrigued by the latter two commodities for I had noticed that several of the cobbled streets leading up to the plaza had been decorated in various religious motifs formed by sprinkling the flower petals onto the cobbled street.

As we walked up calle La Paz, approaching the plaza, the decorations increased in number and complexity; the colours becoming more vivid and the shapes within the decorations more intricate. There were many stalls now near the plaza and I asked an elderly lady sitting next to her stall what was the occasion for such decorations.

"Why, Señor" she replied, "it is usual on this Sunday for the priests to bless the animals and carriages of the people. Later in the day after Mass, the priest will come and bless all of the animals and the carts of their owners, even the handcarts!" she laughed.

"Thank you, Mother." I replied "but what are the purposes of the small jugs of chicha? Surely it is not for the priests?"

The old lady's deep brown lined face was split with a huge grin.

"Oh no, Señor! the priests or the owners take the chicha and after the priest has sprinkled holy water onto their cart, the owners will pour a little chicha onto their carts or animals so that some of it will fall to the ground. It is to honour

Pachamama[7] and so give some extra meaning to the blessing. Of course, what the owners and the priests do with it afterwards is their own affair," she said with a chuckle.

I thanked the old lady who no doubt thought that we were uncouth strangers not to be aware of such local customs. We walked across the neat plaza which is planted with many shade trees and has a beautiful statue of a young woman at its centre. In front of the imposing white basilica with its coloured and patterned domes and brown edging, was a long line of several more stalls, all decked with garlands of many colours and a great variety of other trinkets. Julio and I decided that we would visit these after Mass. Up the few steps we walked into the forecourt of the basilica, passing a rather grand statue of some robed personage

---

[7] *Pachamama is the old Incan goddess of the Earth and fertility. The rite of pouring some of one's drink onto the ground is called challa and in many places of the high Andes it is considered good manners to do so when offered a drink. Pachamama is often equated with the Virgin Mary in many rituals.*

near the main entry. Inside, we were struck by the beauty but relative simplicity of the interior, save for the rich altar and a small niche containing a richly decorated stature of the Virgin. The walls of the main nave were painted white, and the supporting columns were yellow. The vaulted domed ceilings were pale blue with a spider-web of arches in orange. The overall effect was most pleasing.

The Mass was given in the usual way by an old priest who gave a spirited sermon on the virtues of gaining strength from the Scriptures. At the end of the Mass, Julio and I waited until most of the faithful had left and I approached the priest who was standing at the entry door farewelling his flock.

"Excuse me, Padre," I said as we came up to the old man "could you please tell me who is the person carved in such a beautiful statue?" and I pointed to the statue which stood just outside of the entryway.

The old priest looked up and then around to see who else was coming out of the nave. Then he looked into my eyes and smiled.

"You are strangers here, I can tell. Why, this is our famous carver, Don Francisco Tito Yupanqui who carved our magnificent stature of our Blessed Virgin of Copacabana who you would have seen inside. She is the patroness of all of Bolivia!"

The old priest, who had introduced himself as Father Sancho, looked at me, smiled and then up at the face of the statue.

"It is a most beautiful statue indeed, Señor. Would you care to hear the story of Don Francisco and the Virgin of Copacabana? I have a little time before my brothers and I must go and bless the animals and their carts."

Father Sancho looked up again at the statue and then out towards the plaza. He sat down upon the broad base of the statue and began the story of Francisco Tito Yupanqui, the carver of the statue of the patroness of Bolivia.

"It was around 1580 when the harvest had been very bad and there had been other calamities as well, so the people had become frightened and wanted some divine help. Despite having received the Christian faith, they were still attached to their original religion but never-the-less some decided to erect a statue and dedicate it to the Virgen de la Candelaria[8]. Unfortunately, the various factions in the town could not decide upon this dedication and so nothing was done." He said, his arms going up in a gesture of hopelessness.

"That is the way of many town committees' I replied in consolation.

"However!", Father Sancho continued, "one man, Francisco Tito Yupanqui, who was born in

_____

[8] *More correctly Nuestra Señora de la Candelaria – Our Lady of the Candles or simply the Virgin of the Candles described in the last story.*

Copacabana but was a descendant of the Inca, Huayna Capac[9] did not abandon the idea and conceived the project of carving an image of the Virgin who would help the people. This amateur sculptor, helped by his brother Felipe, worked the image of the Virgin in clay to represent all of the natural graces of Mary. But alas, they were but poor fishermen and so the image was not very good, and it was placed on one side of the altar by Father Pedro, the parish priest at that time. However, when Father Pedro left the Parish, his successor ordered the poor image to be removed from the church. Francisco Tito, humiliated by this setback, went to Potosí well to our south where he found an outstanding master of sacred images called Diego Ortiz who taught him how to sculpt in wood. With this knowledge he decided to again work on the final image of the Virgin de la Candelaria. Finally, after much opposition from some of the other factions, the statue was finally

---

[9] *Huayna Capac, (Quechua: "the young mighty one" - 1468–1524) was raised in Cuzco and was the eleventh emperor of the Inca civilization.*

brought to Copacabana on the second of February 1583. You see!" said Father Sancho pointing out into the plaza, "we have even named our lovely little plaza to honour the day that the Virgin came to our city - the Plaza 2 de Febrero[10]. Our Virgin is made of dark mahogany wood, so she is often known romantically as La Morena, the Dark Virgin or the Black Madonna."

Father Sancho folded his arms and sat contented, having told his story which explained many questions which had entered my head since arriving in Copacabana.

"Thank you, Padre", I said "have there been any miracles attributed to the Virgin – after all, she is the patroness of your country?"

The old priest looked up with a little sadness in his eyes that such things should be doubted. "Many, my son. Perhaps the most famous one occurred many years later when two men from

[10] *Plaza of the Second of February.*

Brazil visited the city. Not knowing the capricious nature of our lake, they went fishing way out upon its deep waters. You saw yesterday perhaps, how quickly a storm may come up. Yes?"

"Yes, Padre" I replied, "the darkness and lightning were most violent."

"It is true!" continued Father Sancho, "these poor fishermen feared for their lives and prayed that they would be saved. It is said that they saw a vision of the Virgin of Copacabana who guided them safely back to shore. In gratitude, they had a replica of our stature made and took it back to their home country where it was placed into a small chapel near the beach at the city of Rio de Janeiro. Here the chapel received many devotees and so they renamed the barrio in honour of the Virgin of Copacabana and their famous beach now still bears that name. Perhaps this is almost a jest on their fierce Atlantic Ocean when you remember that 'Copacabana' comes from an Aymara phrase 'kota kahuana', which means 'a view of the lake.'"

Story Twelve

The Revenge of the Alligator Man
(La Venganza del Hombre Caimán)

This is a children's story from Colombia and is another of the type of given by parents all around the world to children and in many cultures to warn the young ones from the dangers of going near the water.

Saturday nights were usually very special at Abuela[1] Isabella's house. It was one of the larger houses near the small farming community of Santa Maria not far from the Laguna de la Cocha in south-western Colombia. It was of two storeys, being made of mudbrick, plastered on the outside and painted a light blue. The roof was of tightly woven thatch which kept out the rain, often heavy in these mountains, from coming into the two small rooms of the upper storey. In one corner of the biggest room, Abuelo Luis had made a small cooking place

[1] *Grandmother*

out of mud brick where his wife would cook their meals.

Below, there was a small storeroom and a wide stable with a small stall at the far end for Margareta, Abuelo[2] Luis's tiny mule. Abuelo Luis and his friends had built this house when he was a young man and knew that he would soon marry Isabella, the loveliest girl in the village of El Encano, which is just a few kilometres north of the lake.

Saturday nights were often special for the extended family as all of the adults; the children of the old couple, their children and sometimes old friends of the family, would gather there to drink chicha[3] beer or the fiery aguardente[4] which Tío[5] Ramone would get from the nearby town of Pasto. Abuela Isabella would often

[2] *Grandfather*
[3] *A beer of the Andes made from corn. It is alcoholic if fermented.*
[4] *A fiery spirit – literally 'fire water' and is an anise-flavoured liqueur derived from sugarcane, popular in the Andean region*
[5] *Uncle*

make up a large batch of Champús, especially near Christmas time. It was made from crushed maize in addition to panela[6], lulo[7], pineapple, cinnamon, cloves and orange tree leaves. This drink or the unfermented chicha was always in plentiful supply on Saturday nights for the children, along with tasty morsels from the kitchen including patacones[8], empanades[9] and cocadas[10].

There would always be a crowd of people coming to visit and tonight was no exception. Tío Maximiliano, Abuela Isabella's son and Bobo her grandson, who lived nearby, would come early in the evening for dinner. Before it got dark, Tío Maximiliano would cut some timber from the scant wood heap outside and generally do some of the little necessities of maintenance around the house whilst Bobo

[6] *Unrefined, whole cane sugar sold in blocks.*
[7] *An exotic fruit with a citrus flavour Solanum quitoense.*
[8] *Fried green plantains.*
[9] *Pasties filled with meat and/or vegetables.*
[10] *Coconut balls.*

would go and talk to his grandfather in the upstairs room used for dining and general daily use. They got on well, did Abuelo Luis and Bobo; poor Abuelo Luis was not up for long and deep discussions, and these were also equally beyond Bobo's mind. Abuelo Luis would sit in the old, ragged armchair and talk with his grandson. They talked about horses mainly, which was Abuelo Luis's only passion and what the weekly newspaper said about the form of various starters in the upcoming horse races at the Hipódromo de Los Andes north of Bogota.

Usually, dinner was a very informal affair on most nights at the house with Tío Maximiliano and Abuelo Isabella sitting on one side of the big, scrubbed pine table and Abuelo Luis and Bobo at each end. The table had been pressed up hard against the wall and was usually the repository of various sundry items needing attention, such as shopping bags, and lists of groceries, letters and other items of mail, all sorts of paraphernalia for knitting and sewing, including work clothes that Tío Maximiliano always seemed to bring home on many occasions for his mother to wash. However, sometime before setting the table, these items would be cleared out of the way, often onto the bed in the other upstairs room.

Around eight in the evening, Abuela Isabella would serve up la cena[11]; usually something light such as empanadas, sometimes with aborrajado[12]. The main meal of the day was el almuerzo[13], usually taken in the middle of the day which often included rice or potatoes, arepas[14], red beans, a piece of beef, chicken or fish with sometimes plantains. The food of the almuerzo was usually served with a fresh fruit juice or 'jugo'. Often at meals, Bobo seemed to have missed the lesson, given many a time by his Abuela, about talking with one's mouth full

---

[11] *Dinner*

[12] *A **sweet treat** consisting of cheese-stuffed sweet plantain slices that are battered and deep-fried.*

[13] *Lunch*

[14] *is a type of flatbread made of ground maize dough stuffed with a rich filling.*

and so his eating habits reminded her of the rotating mass of tangled clothing seen when she did the washing in her old tub. Poor Abuela Isabella! She had long since given up teaching Bobo some manners, but at least sometimes he did try – on occasions - lunch not being one of them.

After dinner, Abuela Isabella would clear the table and take the dishes downstairs to the bench under the covered stair to wash them, sometimes with Bobo's help but mostly not. Tío Ramone would also go downstairs and sit on the last step of the old wooden staircase and smoke much to his mother's disgust as she thought that it was a disgusting habit even though most of the local men also followed the habit. Even Abuelo Luis once liked to smoke a cigar in the evening until his wife suggested that he should stop. Wives often act this way in the best interests of their husbands, even in Colombia!

Saturday night was a special night as it was card night and many of the old couple's relatives and some friends would come over to play tute,[15] or some other card game. It was more of a social event than a gambling spree; the players would often play for tokens or even a few coins if Tío Ramone came. Now here was a man with a gambling habit; he would bet on two cockroaches climbing up a wall if there was someone silly enough to take the bet. Abuela Isabella often hinted that he may also be involved at selling illegal lottery tickets, but who knows?

Tío Ramone would also come early on those Saturday nights and he and his brother Maximiliano would go to the corner of the walled yard at the back of the house to where there was a large circular ring of stones covered with old boards and sacks and logs to keep them lifting off in the wind. Tío Maximiliano would remove the covering to open up an old

[15] *A popular card game played by families and is a trick-taking card game of the ace–ten families for two to four players played with Spanish playing cards.*

water well revelling it as a deep and dark circular pit lined with stone. Not far down was a black pool of water.

He stood up and reached for a long rope which ran down the closest wall of the well and into the dark water below and began hauling it up. Soon a rather shapeless mass of a rough canvas bag slowly emerged from the water. It made a strange clinking sound as it pulled it up the stony side of the well. Pulling the bag out of the well and onto the ground, he untied the strong leather cord which was threaded around the lip of the bag and extracted several large brown, tightly-stoppered jugs. Chicha!

"This will do for a while, "he said and retied the bag and lowered it carefully back into the well. Sliding back the covering, he gave Ramone a sly wink and they returned to the house. So, this was where the family kept its homemade corn beer! Back in the kitchen, Tío Maximiliano opened one of the jugs and poured a little into an earthenware beaker and handed it to his brother. He also poured a generous amount into his glass, raised it on high and said:

"Salud!"

The old well had long since been used as a source of drinking water. Now it was used for another purpose for drinking, and it kept all that went into the canvas bag extremely cold.

The sun had now set, back into the house, as the other guests had started to arrive. In those days, when people visited on such an occasion as this, the entire family would also go. There would be enough food and drink set out on the big table in the dining room upstairs and everyone would eat, drink and talk to their family and friends. Soon, the children would go downstairs to the big room below, pat Margareta the mule and perhaps give her a treat such as an apple. Of course, the rest of this room would have been cleaned earlier in the day by Tío Maximiliano and Bobo; the bundles of hay pushed back to the far walls and the clay floor swept clean. Tío Maximiliano would unroll an old length of carpet to cover the floor, and the old table used for all of Abuelo Luis's constructions, would be dragged out to the centre of the room. It was then covered in a neat tablecloth and jugs of unfermented chicha and other party delicacies for the children were brought down from the kitchen above.

The adults would stay in the main room upstairs with Bobo and his other older cousins being given the task of looking after the younger children downstairs.

As all of the chairs had been taken to the upstairs room, the floor of the large room below was spread with rugs and sacks for the children to sit upon. This was not to be for Bobo, as he held supreme as the leader of the 'big boys' who were there, including Prima[16] Ximena whose female gender was usually discounted in Bobo's concept hierarchy. She was an intelligent and

16 *Prima is a female cousin, Primo being the male version.*

caring girl who usually kept a maternal eye on what the younger kids got up to.

On this night, all of the adults settled themselves upstairs around the dining room table, as was the custom, their beakers filled with chicha or aguardiente and the playing cards were produced. Downstairs, with the children all sitting on rugs or sacks up against the side wall, Bobo turned down the old oil lamp which hung from the ceiling over the table which left the large room in its faint yellow glow. The shadows on the wall gave the entire room an eerie scene of foreboding. Little Prima Sofia, who was all of four years of age cuddled up to Prima Ximena who was furthest from the table. Bobo did not help matters by jumping up and sitting on the table, bathed in the flickering glow like fiend from the darkness outside.

Bobo was in his element now leering down at the younger children; the older ones knew what to expect and all grinned expectedly. Bobo was now the teller of tales, as he leaned closer to the edge of the table and said in a quiet but mysterious tone:

"Tonight, I'll tell you of the tale of the El Hombre Caimán[17] of the Laguna de la Cocha."

There was a shudder amongst the littlies and a stifled laugh from the oldsters because everyone in the town knew of the Alligator Man. The lake was not far from the back of the house as Abuelo Luis thought that it would be handy for fishing and drawing water for his meagre crops. It was a big lake, the second largest in the country, in fact and it had formed in the remains of a large, extinct volcanic crater.

Bobo went on to tell the story of the half man – half alligator who inhabited the lake. It was an old legend and had come other parts of Colombia and Bobo had heard it somewhere

[17] *The Alligator Man – a Caimán is not exactly an alligator but belongs to the sub-family* **Caimaninae**, *of the Alligatoridae family these are common in Central and South America.*

and tonight had decided to make it a local legend.

With the low light of the lamp, Bobo recounted the legend of the Alligator Man in as much horrific detail as his fertile imagination could conjure up. He told of the once shy young man who was too timid, and only dared to watch the local young maidens from a distance.

"Very much like you, Antonio!" Bobo said, pointing to one of the younger boys who now sat well back from the table. The older boys laughed at their cousin's embarrassment.

Bobo continued his story about how the young maidens often went down to the lake's shore to wash their clothing and the shy young man wanted to secretly get closer to them. Alas, the shore around the lake where they did the washing was open and bare and they would see him as he approached. He needed to get closer to them and his frustration grew into an obsession. Finally in despair, he summoned up enough courage to go to an old Brujo[18] who lived up in the hills which surrounded the lake. Reluctant at first, the old Brujo, who well knew about loneliness, warned the young man that he could help him but to do as he what he desired, he would have to be turned into a caimán so that he would swim silently and undetected right up to where the young maidens washed their clothing at the edge of the lake. He gave the shy young man two small jars containing potions; one was red and this would turn the shy young man into a caimán and the other was white which would turn him back into a man.

So, early one morning as he saw several young maidens carrying their washing down to the lake, he crept up as close as he could and, leaving the white potion on a rock nearby, he drank the red potion.

"Uuuugh! Uuuugh!" Bobo gasped, clutching his throat and twisting his body around, first in one

[18] *Witch Doctor*

direction and then the other as though he was the shy young man going through the agony of his body changing into that of a caimán. Using the faint light of the lamp, he then made a moving shadow on the far wall using his hands clasped together like the opening and closing jaws of a caimán.

Little Sofia was scared by the noises and the fierce shadow and snuggled even closer into Prima Ximena.

Bobo went on to say in the most extravagant of terms how the shy young man, now in the shape of a caimán, went back to the rock where he had left the other jug of potion so that he could once more become a man. But alas! He had only taken one small sip when the jug fell out of his ungainly caimán claws and was dashed to pieces on the rock. His body began to change but only the top half; the bottom half remaining as the hindquarters and tail of a caimán. So now he was condemned to live in the lake, only coming out at night to hunt for his prey – even little children – Bobo emphasised with some glee. The only joy which the Alligator Man now had was the playing of his small siku[19] which is often mistaken for the sound of a caimán breathing.

"It's the truth!" said Bobo indignantly, "because Papa Marco told me so and he's an old Kamsá[20] man who lives in the hills and knows everything.

Little Sofia cuddled even closer to Prima Ximena and the some of the younger children looked about the room and out into the darkness beyond the small wall and towards the lake.

"Toot! Toot! Tooty! Toot!" Bobo made the soft and eerie sounds of his version of the sound of a siku with his lips.

The youngsters all cowed as Bobo swept his hand across the little group on the floor. The

[19] *Pan pipes common to many people of the Andes*
[20] *One of the local indigenous peoples who live around the Laguna de la Cocha.*

older boys again stifled a laugh, and little Sofia began to cry.

Now, with a quite few glasses of chicha in them, there were thoughts in some young minds of going to the toilet. This was absolutely the very last option for the younger children and even some of the older boys who had taken some of Bobo's dramatic explanations to heart.

Going to the outhouse at night had always been a problem for the children at the farmhouse. Abuelo Luis had built a sturdy baño[21] a short distance from the main building further down near the lake so that the large drum of water placed outside could be easily refilled. It was reached by a small track which went from the back gate down to its doorway. At night there was always a candle and a tinder box with tapers in a small alcove at the bottom of the stairs to light the way. It was always a scary adventure for the older children on most nights

[21] *Toilet*

and the younger ones usually went with an adult. Tonight however, after Bobo's elaborate descriptions of the fierce Alligator Man, no one dared to venture out into the darkness of the lake's shore.

Bobo had finished his story about the Alligator Man of Laguna de la Cocha and leaned back to down another glass of chicha. Little Sofia had buried herself into the coat of Prima Ximena and some of the other younger children were looking about with some apprehension thinking whether or not their need to go to the toilet was worth the risk of being taken by the monster. It could have easily slithered up from the lake having heard young voices in the farmhouse.

Seeing their distress and getting a little joy from his impact on the youngsters, Bobo now proudly boasted in a casual way that he was not afraid of any such creature and was going out for a short 'break' and that he would kick the tale of the Alligator Man should he be encountered. With that, he got up, lit the small candle, which was nearby and dramatically strode out of the room and through the back gate and out into Alligator Man territory.

Now as it happened, Tío Ramone had heard the whole of Bobo's story and the effects that it had on the younger children. He had come down as usual to sit on the first step of the stairs in the darkness to smoke his cigar. After Bobo left to go out to the toilet, he threw his cigar away and went into the room where the children now sat uncertain as to what the rest of the night would bring. He saw little Sofia crying cuddled up to prima Ximena. He asked her what was wrong, and she exclaimed:

"Aw! Silly Primo Bobo scared the wits out of her with his story about the Alligator Man and he's gone out to el baño and has left the gate open."

"Oh, has he?" said Tío Ramone a wicked gleam in his eye as he gave the older boys a wink. His slicked back dark hair parted in the middle, a thin black moustache and gaunt face made him look like some caricature of the devil which was painted on the walls of the little church in the village. He did not say anything but turned about and went back upstairs to where the other adults were playing cards.

As he went into the room, he gave a brief nod to Abuelo Luis and said "I'll just borrow the siku which you have hanging on the wall over there. I thought that I would try to play it with the children downstairs."

Now Tío Ramone was in fact an accomplished player of the siku in his youth and now he thought that he would put it to another use other than playing for the children downstairs. He quietly went down the stairs, turned and went out the front gate of the yard.

There was another small track going down to the lake past the old yard which Abuelo Luis kept Margareta in the warmer months. This bypassed the outhouse where a small glimmer of light showed that Bobo was enthroned.

Going around the outhouse very quietly, he crept up from the direction of the lake, the typical route that any self-respecting, child-eating Alligator Man would take. Not far from the little building, he stood up and putting the siku to his lips played:

"Toot! Toot! Tooty! Toot!" and then a more eerie and soft melody like that of a caimán breathing.

The door of the outhouse burst open, and a terrified Bobo came screaming out and ran up the track to the house, his pants still about his knees and a flurry of straw left in his wake.

The revenge of the Alligator Man had been taken.

About the Author

Raised and educated in Sydney, Australia, he graduated as a High School Science Teacher and later achieved a Bachelor of Science, Master's degrees in Science, (Geology) and Educational Administration and a Doctorate in Education.

A specialist in the Earth Sciences, he took his chosen field seriously and has visited all seven continents including travelling in South America where his daughter-in-law's family live. Here he and his wife travelled extensively in the high Andes and also to many of the places mentioned in this book.

He now lives in Brisbane, Australia with his wife and their sons and families and their grandchildren. He is the author of over twenty books on Earth Science, Environmental Science and several works of fiction.

Dr Scott at Baños de Agua Santa, Ecuador 2011

www.ingramcontent.com/pod-product-compliance
Lightning Source LLC
Chambersburg PA
CBHW071752190726
48292CB00003B/953